"The Focus Of My Life Isn't Sex,"

Maggie said firmly.

"So you've sworn off anything that's remotely sensual." Mick rolled off the bed, a towel clasped loosely around his lean hips. Unconsciously, Maggie took a pace backward.

He smiled coldly. "Don't look so scared. I'll leave you alone now. I had to find out something, that's all. I needed to make sure you were telling the truth. Forgive my methods."

"Your *methods*!" Maggie sputtered. "You mean you were playacting just now?"

"To see how you'd react. Sure."

"Why, you—big thug!"

He grinned, bracing his bare shoulder against the doorframe. "It's not polite to call people names." He wagged one finger at her. "You've got a hell of a suspicious setup here. It's my business to separate truth from fiction."

"Did kissing me solve your dilemma?"

"It helped."

Dear Reader:

Welcome! You hold in your hand a Silhouette Desire—your ticket to a whole new world of reading pleasure.

A Silhouette Desire is a sensuous, contemporary romance about passions, problems and the ultimate power of love. It is about today's woman—intelligent, successful, giving—but it is also the story of a romance between two people who are strong enough to follow their own individual paths, yet strong enough to compromise, as well.

These books are written by, for and about every woman that you are—wife, mother, sister, lover, daughter, career woman. A Silhouette Desire heroine must face the same challenges, achieve the same successes, in her story as you do in your own life.

The Silhouette reader is not afraid to enjoy herself. She knows when to take things seriously and when to indulge in a fantasy world. With six books a month, Silhouette Desire strives to meet her many moods, but each book is always a compelling love story.

Make a commitment to romance—go wild with Silhouette Desire!

Best,

Isabel Swift
Senior Editor & Editorial Coordinator

NANCY MARTIN
Hit
Man

Silhouette Desire

Published by Silhouette Books New York

America's Publisher of Contemporary Romance

SILHOUETTE BOOKS
300 East 42nd St., New York, N.Y. 10017

ISBN: 0-373-05461-0

First Silhouette Books printing November 1988

Printed in the U.S.A.

Books by Nancy Martin

Silhouette Intimate Moments

Black Diamonds #60

Silhouette Desire

Hit Man #461

NANCY MARTIN

has lived in a succession of small towns in Pennsylvania, though she loves to travel to find locations for romance in larger cities in this country and abroad. Now she lives with her husband, two daughters and an overly exuberant retriever in a house they've restored and are constantly tinkering with.

If Nancy's not sitting at her word processor with a stack of records on the stereo, you might find her cavorting with her children, skiing with her husband or relaxing by the pool. She loves writing romances and has also written as Elissa Curry.

One

Children screaming jolted Maggie Kincaid out of her doze. Startled that she'd actually fallen asleep, she was off her beach chair and onto her feet before she was even fully alert—the lioness instinct, a mother's chemical reaction to her worst fears. *This was it!*

But the screams turned to shrieks of laughter, and Maggie sagged against the balcony balustrade in relief. Weakly, she waved down at her daughter Elizabeth, glad to see the five-year-old skip happily over the incoming surf and land with a splash in the rippling foam of the backwash. For the past few days Elizabeth had been terribly homesick, but now a new light of pleasure glowed on her small face as the warm Caribbean bubbled around her ankles.

"Mama! Look!" she cried, pushing her straw hat off her forehead and sending a gap-toothed smile up to the terrace. "I found a friend! A *friend*!"

Sure enough, a raven-haired little boy cavorted in the water next to Elizabeth. He was a sprite from the sea—brown from the sun and naked as a jaybird. Next to Elizabeth's slender daintiness he looked a satyr in miniature, complete with bare bottom and a cocky stance. He turned to glare up at the terrace, shading his eyes against the brilliant dazzle of afternoon sunlight.

"I'm thirsty!" he bellowed at Maggie, as if she were to blame for his condition.

Maggie laughed. Clearly, etiquette was not the strong suit of this brash rascal. "Bring him up, Elizabeth," she called, feeling generous after her scare. "There's lemonade."

At the mere mention of a treat, the two children cheered and bounded for the zigzag path of stone stairs that led from the beach to the terrace of the Kincaid villa. Built on the ruins of a fortress belonging to a 19th-century pirate who called himself the Scourge of Something-or-Other, the modern portion of the villa jutted from the cliff-side by some architectural miracle and soared over its own private stretch of curving Caribbean beach. The ocean provided a spectacular azure panorama on three sides, and a practically impenetrable tangle of mountain jungle lay on the fourth. Closer at hand on the terrace, it was climbing roses not pillaging buccaneers that rampaged across the balustrade and onto a trellis over the French doors. A scattering of expensive wrought-iron furniture, a frosty pitcher of lemonade, Maggie's collection of papers, a notebook and a snoozing Siamese cat completed the set.

And it could have been a movie set, Maggie mused as she turned her back on the beach to survey her sun-washed surroundings. But only such chic cinematic aristocrats as Cary Grant or Grace Kelly could have lounged with the right degree of élan among the potted flowers on the battlements. Valhalla meets Palm Beach, Maggie had always thought of the place. A far cry from her usual staid New England haunts. But it was surprisingly peaceful. The perfect spot to forget one's troubles and relax.

Except Maggie wasn't relaxing. Or forgetting. Three days of hiding at the villa with Elizabeth had only served to heighten Maggie's anxiety. She hadn't let Elizabeth out of her sight. Even as her daughter pounded up the last of the steps with her naked little friend in tow, Maggie wondered if she had made a mistake.

"Mama, this is Spider! He's just my age!"

Elizabeth skidded to a stop on the flagstones, and her bare-bottomed companion swaggered confidently behind. His round little face remained impassive and proud, and Maggie saw his wicked black eyes scoot this way and that as he sized up the place. He halted, cocked his fists on his hips and so resembled a conquering pirate king for a split second that Maggie had to laugh.

She smothered the impulse quickly and greeted the boy as politely as if he were royalty indeed. "Hello, Spider. We're delighted you could be our guest."

"I'm not staying," he announced, lordly as you please in spite of the fact that his front teeth were missing. "I'm only getting a drink."

"I see," said Maggie. "Will you have a seat? May I offer you a towel?"

He accepted one of the plush mauve towels, but circumvented Maggie's intention by dropping it onto one of the chairs and proceeding to sit on it rather than covering himself. Elizabeth, Maggie noted, seemed avidly intrigued by her new friend's unusual anatomy. Her daughter had been too sheltered, Maggie decided. If she wasn't careful, Elizabeth was going to grow up as Victorian as her mother.

"Spider's a *boy*, Mama," Elizabeth said firmly, seating herself on the chair next to his and primly clasping her hands on her knees. "He's five and he collects tarantulas."

"Goodness," said Maggie, already pouring the lemonade into tall glasses. "You've obviously learned a lot about each other in just a few minutes. Are you staying nearby, Spider?"

He took the glass and noisily gulped some lemonade before answering. "Nope," he said, wiping his mouth with the back of his sandy hand. "My dad and I have a yacht. We're passing through, that's all."

Maggie frowned. She hadn't figured on trouble arriving by sea. The villa was nicely isolated otherwise. With a glance out at the water, Maggie saw not just one but two boats anchored within shouting distance. One was a large, lavishly outfitted yacht, and closer to shore lay a small, low-lying sailboat, somewhat battered but graceful as she bobbed in the water.

"Which boat is yours, Spider?" Elizabeth asked eagerly. "The big one or the little one?"

Spider's chest swelled. "Oh, the big one," he replied. "We're very rich."

But Maggie had seen his quick eyes flicker and knew he was lying. At that moment she decided that Spider could definitely be categorized as a "pistol."

The cat got up from her nap in the sunshine, stretched, took note of the newcomer with regal indifference and leaped onto Maggie's bare thighs. Maggie gathered up the animal automatically. "Does your father know you're up here?" she asked, smoothing the cat's fur.

"Sure. He told me to play on the beach while he got the boat ready for the storm."

"Storm?"

"Yeah, a hurricane. It's going to hit any minute."

Maggie glanced at the sky. Not a cloud in sight. Controlling another smile, she asked, "Will he be worried if he can't see you?"

"Oh, no," said Spider. "He knows I can take care of myself. You got any cookies?"

"We don't eat between meals, Spider," Elizabeth chided. "Why don't you tell Mama about the sharks?"

"Sharks?" asked Maggie. Certain that she shouldn't believe a word that came out of the boy's mouth. She was content to humor him. "What about the sharks?"

"Oh, that was nothing," scoffed Spider. He put his bare feet up on the edge of the glass table and wiggled his chubby toes. "We got surrounded by a whole herd of man-eaters, but my dad shot 'em."

"He shot a herd of sharks?"

"Yeah," said Spider, yawning hugely. "With a revolver. My dad's a crack shot."

"He does contracts," Elizabeth volunteered knowledgeably.

"Contracts?"

"Yeah, you know," said Spider. "You want to take out a contract on somebody, you call my old man."

"He works for a mob!" Elizabeth added.

"Elizabeth," Maggie began, "you shouldn't say things like—you mean he works for a *Mob*?"

"*The* Mob," Spider corrected. "My dad can ice anybody you want iced. He's a whiz at all the tough stuff—kneecaps, amputations. Sometimes even wiretaps and bodyguard work. Anything you want done, my dad can do it." He drained his drink, then slid his eyes suspiciously toward Maggie. "You sure you don't have cookies?"

"Sorry," said Maggie faintly, staring at the little monster. "We're fresh out."

"Hmm." He frowned. Then, to make them understand who they were dealing with, he proceeded to balance the empty glass on the end of his thumb and declared suddenly. "I've eaten ants before."

"Really?" Elizabeth gasped.

"Yep. And a snake once, too."

"H—how?" Elizabeth asked, leaning forward.

Spider gave up trying to balance the glass and shrugged nonchalantly. "With catsup, of course."

By that time Maggie was debating the best way to shoo the unsavory little urchin off her terrace, when a breeze from the ocean brought to their ears a terrible roar—the belligerent shout of an angered father.

"Spider!"

At the sound of his incensed parent, Spider scrambled off his chair, his face the picture of utter terror.

The father must have seen the zigzag path and the terrace above and assumed it was the only way his son could have come, because he shot up the path two steps at a time and arrived on the terrace like a famished tiger springing from the underbrush. The cat on Maggie's lap gave a startled meow and leaped for safety behind the rose trellis.

He was as tall and dark as Mephistopheles, with flashing black eyes, wild curly black hair and three days' worth of stubble on his jutting jaw. A sheen of seawater glistened on his body, and for a split second Maggie thought he'd come naked as the boy. In the next instant, though, she realized he was bare-chested but wearing a pair of soaked cutoff twill trousers that were plastered against his body and rode low on his lean hips. If his son had appeared with the lordly air of a conquering hero, then the father was Mars, the Roman god of war, bristling with hostility and carrying the fire of imminent combat in his eyes. He had Spider's fallen-angel face, but his was also harder—heavier browed, tight-lipped and totally lacking in naiveté. Judging by the asymmetrical nature of his face, he'd broken his nose a time or two, probably in street brawls. All in all, a magnificent specimen of rampant male animal.

"What the hell have you been doing?" he demanded.

Spider faced his father, and Maggie expected the boy to cringe in terror before this specter of parental wrath.

But little Spider stood his ground. "I'm havin' a drink," he replied, matching his father's belligerence decibel for decibel. "I was thirsty!"

"There's water in the boat, you little sneak." His father took a menacing pace forward. "I warned you about wandering off! I ought to tan your hide for—"

"I'm afraid it's our fault," Maggie intervened, trying to sound composed, though her heart had somehow lurched into her throat. In the course of her patrician Yankee existence, she had never encountered a genuine hit man face-to-face. Cautiously she got to her feet. "We coaxed Spider to accept our hospitality. Please don't be angry with him."

The man skewered Maggie with a look that clearly suggested she was a a liar—and more. His accent was pure Brooklyn. "Who the hell are you?"

"My name is Margaret Kincaid. This is my daughter, Elizabeth."

He glanced in Elizabeth's direction, but swung back and narrowed his black eyes to study Maggie's face. Then his gaze slipped lower. Until that moment Maggie hadn't given a thought to her attire—a sleek white maillot hastily bought at an airport boutique. But the expression that dawned in the eyes of Spider's father made her wish she'd chosen something more her usual style—something covered up and completely proper. The fact that she hadn't yet spent enough time in the sun to develop a tan made her feel pale and even more exposed—hardly the gentle lady from New England. In fact, Maggie probably looked as if she'd gone AWOL from Club Med.

The corners of the man's mouth twitched, his brows rose and his dark eyes filled with sparkle in an unmistakable what-have-we-here look.

To keep herself from blushing, Maggie summoned her mistress-of-the-manor voice. "May I ask your name?"

"Spiderelli," he said, allowing a slow grin to appear as he extended his right hand. "Mick Spiderelli."

She had no choice but to accept the handshake of a professional thug. His grip was warm and solid, and the strength of it somehow forced Maggie to look into his face. Their gazes met and held as if magnetically attracted. Not just a thug, Maggie thought, but a womanizing thug, as well. The bemused look on his face prompted Maggie to wonder what kind of first impression she must have been giving him. She could only guess at the picture she made—a small woman with fine English-rose skin, soft gray eyes and dark hair, usually cut and arranged sleekly, but now pulled haphazardly up into an elfin topknot. Her bathing suit was cut absurdly high over slender hips, and her narrow gold necklace had slid into the lightly perspiring valley between her breasts.

Maggie determined to set him straight. She was no aging surfer girl. Coolly, she said, "How do you do?" With a wave at the pitcher and glasses, she asked, "Would you care for a lemonade?"

Like his son, Spiderelli absorbed the setting with a quick, assessing glance. He took in the crystal glassware, the sheaf of embossed notepaper on the table and Maggie's monogrammed gold pen—all subtle but certain signs of wealth. Though the villa's long windows were curtained against the blazing sunshine, he could easily see through the gauzy material to the airy salon with its marble floor, white baby grand and the glint of a gilt-framed Italian mirror. Strains of recorded Mozart floated on the air.

Like an expert pickpocket, he summed up the situation and calculated his chances for success. With a full-fledged grin on his face, he returned his vivid gaze to Maggie and said, "I don't like lemonade much. You got any beer around?"

Maggie bit down on her back teeth and mustered a fairly good imitation of a smile. "There might be some in the refrigerator."

He pulled a slouchy baseball cap from his hip pocket and settled it over his too-long hair. The shapeless cap was emblazoned with the Mets' logo, and Maggie could see he wore it with pride. Giving her a wink, he said, "A beer'd be good."

She figured it might be. But Maggie had been trained to be a lady at all times, and she clung to her creed. "Fine," she said stiffly. "Won't you sit down? I'll go check the kitchen."

Elizabeth piped up. "Can we go back to the beach?"

"Yeah," said Spider. "I want to catch a jellyfish."

"They're dangerous!" Elizabeth cried.

"Not if you know what you're doing," Spider replied with disdain. He tossed his towel at his father and made a grab for Elizabeth's hand. "C'mon. I'll show you."

"Be careful," Maggie cautioned—but too late. The children were gone, scampering down the zigzag toward the sand and surf. Spider's father looped the towel around his shoulders, went to the balustrade and leaned his hands there to watch the children go. "Stay out of the water!" he shouted.

"Yes, sir," Elizabeth called back.

Watching the kids dash off, Mick Spiderelli figured his son had mischief on his mind, so he kept his eye on Spider until both kids were safely on the beach and innocently playing in the sand. Then he turned around to talk to the mother again and discovered she'd disappeared—escaped to the house to look for beer. With a shrug, Mick figured that was his invitation to have a look around.

Barefoot and with the towel around his neck, Mick brushed through the long curtains of the French doors and let out a soft whistle. "Holy smoke," he said aloud. "What a joint!"

He ambled through a cool, elegantly furnished salon to a corridor where a collection of broad swords was hung on permanent display, probably in case Long John Silver should arrive and find need for weaponry. He heard someone banging around farther ahead, so he went down a set of wide stone steps and found himself entering the kitchen. Located in a part of the villa that must have been a fortress at one time, the kitchen resembled a medieval relic that had been made over by interior decorators from San Francisco. Smooth tile countertops, a microwave oven, refrigerator, a double sink and racks and racks of wine contrasted dramatically with the hulking walls built from massive rock. A skylight permitted the afternoon sun to cast a golden swath of light through the bottled wine and create a mosaic on the stone floor. Overhead, a Casablanca fan whirled lazily. In startling contrast, however, a cannon was mounted over the dishwasher, aimed out one of the huge windows that overlooked the ocean.

In a splash of sunlight, Margaret Kincaid was rummaging in the vegetable crisper of the restaurant-sized refrigerator. She came up with a bottle of Michelob, turned around and gasped when she saw him in the doorway.

He had that effect on a lot of women, but Mick figured he'd put her at ease. "This is some swell layout."

The Kincaid woman backed up fast and collided with the counter. Mick lounged down the steps and strolled into the kitchen, checking out the place with the casual air of an interested buyer of exotic real estate. He tipped his Mets' cap back to get a better look around. "I feel like Vincent Price is going to show up any minute." He nodded at the cannon. "You take security seriously around here, don't you?"

"Yes," she said. "But that one's just for show."

Mick grinned. "Thanks for the warning." He sauntered closer and pulled the beer from her grasp. Effortlessly, he twisted off the cap and took a quick, thirsty slug directly from the bottle. Then he gestured to indicate the entire villa. "Your place?"

"My uncle's," she answered, cautiously retreating behind the cooking island. A fine-boned, petite woman with wide gray eyes and cameo skin, she looked shy and thoroughly intimidated. Mick was used to that reaction. She was an easy mark. A ripe and tender morsel, for sure. Her husband was probably a big-city fat cat—too busy conquering Wall Street and keeping his mistress happy to join his family on vacation. The woman was essentially defenseless, reduced to invoking the name of an uncle for protection. Nervously, she said, "Hadn't we better go back to the children?"

"In a minute. They're safe. Your uncle built this place?"

"Well, no." She glanced toward the door. "This was a fort to begin with. A movie star bought it in the forties. Maureen Swansdown, if you remember her."

"Yeah," he said after another sip. "I remember. A real dish. You related to her?"

"By marriage only. A cousin of mine was her husband. Remodeling this fortress nearly bankrupted the Swansdowns, so my uncle bailed them out and bought it."

"Your uncle an oil baron or something?"

"No," she said with precision. "He's in the newspaper business."

Mick grinned. "His name isn't Hearst, by any chance?"

"No," she said again, and drew herself up with a show of pride and defiance. "Kincaid is the name. J. B. Kincaid. He—the family owns newspapers on the East Coast."

"The New York Times?"

"No, smaller papers. Philadelphia's *Daily Post*, the *Hartford Herald*, Boston's *Sun Gazette*."

"I get the idea," Mick said easily. Not impressed by her invocation of blue-blooded publishers, he pulled out one of the stools from the island and sat on it, bracing his forearms on the counter and cradling the icy beer in both hands. "So who are you?" he asked casually. "The idle rich niece of a newspaper magnate? Or do you have a job in the real world?"

"I'm not idle and I'm not rich," she said. "I work for the papers, too."

He glanced down her body. He couldn't stop himself, really. "You must do a lot for the office decor."

That did it. She reached for an oversize powder-pink cotton shirt she'd left slung over one of the stools. Rapidly, she put on the flowing garment over her bathing suit. Fastening the buttons, she said, "I'm not just there for decoration. I pull my own weight. I'm a writer."

He sipped his beer and regretfully watched her progress with the buttons. "Reporter?"

"No. I'm a columnist. Shall we go back outside?"

"What kind of columnist?"

"Really, the children are—"

"Let me guess," he said, making no move to leave. "You write for the society pages."

She shook her head. "No. That's my cousin Priscilla's beat."

"Well, then?"

Her eyes snapped with fire. "I do fashion," she said sharply. "Fashion and . . ."

"And what?"

"Etiquette," she said, giving in reluctantly. "I'm Dear Miss Margaret."

He laughed, of course, and lifted his bottle in a kind of salute. "I shoulda guessed," he said. "You certainly look the type."

Blushing, she spun away and finished buttoning up her shirt by fastening the last one tight against her throat. Goading her was pretty good sport. "You gonna correct my manners?" Mick asked, grinning. "Make me watch my p's and q's?"

"I'm not a traffic cop," she retorted.

"I bet you sure stop traffic now and then, though, don't you?" Laughing, Mick switched his baseball cap around so that the bill shaded the back of his neck and he could get a better view of the picture she made. "Even all covered up like a nun in a church, you sure are easy on the eyes, Miss Margaret."

Her soft gray gaze turned to steel. "Thank you," she said, though curtly.

"You'd rather crack me across the face for that, wouldn't you? But your manners are too good." He chuckled. "Okay, I'll back off. How long have you been down here?"

"A few days."

"Staying long?"

"I'm not sure."

He whistled. "Being the boss's niece must have some advantages. Unlimited vacations—"

"I'm not exactly vacationing," she said, suddenly willing to divulge information. "I write my columns from here. We've got a telex and a phone modem. We're hooked up all over the world for instant communication. You interrupted me, in fact. I was just about to send tomorrow's piece."

Maybe she was telling the truth, but Mick suspected the brag about instant communication was a fib. No doubt she wanted him to think she was a phone call away from a commando rescue invasion. He pretended not to take the hint. "Pretty isolated place you picked to work, though," he observed, "even if you do have your own telex."

"I like my privacy."

A hint didn't come any bigger than that. Mick grinned. "It sure is an unlikely spot for a vacation if you ask me. The kid like privacy, too?"

"Elizabeth? She's—well, she's been a little lonesome, I admit. But she's always been the kind of child to make her own fun. Let's go upstairs now, shall we? I don't like leaving her alone like this."

"Yeah, sure." Mick stood up slowly and stretched.

When he uncoiled himself and stood, smiling at her and oozing Mediterranean charm, Maggie found herself appraising the man suspiciously. He was halfway good-looking behind the stubble, she noted; not a stereotypical hoodlum. With a strong Italian face—proud nose, wide mouth, dark eyes with wonderfully thick lashes that drooped enough to lend a sensual sort of languor to his expression, he looked more like a Roman statue than a hired gun. By the flecks of gray hair at his temples, the weathered crinkles around his eyes and the deep-cut lines that ran from nose to mouth, she guessed his age to be closer to forty than she'd first surmised. Still, he had an intriguing face. And his body—narrow-hipped and broad-shouldered—could have captured the attention of Maggie's ninety-year-old grandmother. The sunshine from the skylight gleamed on his splendid shoulders.

Maggie brought herself up short. Good grief! Not since her college days had she actually ogled a man of any kind, let alone this modern version of Stanley Kowalski. For years she had held herself above the embarrassing skirmishes of the sexual revolution, and now she couldn't seem to tear her eyes from the specimen lounging against her kitchen counter. When she found herself checking out his left hand for a ring—none there—Maggie blushed.

But the telephone cut short her embarrassment. From the wall just over the dishwasher, the phone gave a jangle that nearly sent Maggie rocketing out of her skin. She jumped like a hare, then froze, totally torn about what to do.

"Phone," said Spiderelli mildly.

It rang a second time, and Maggie didn't move.

"Aren't you gonna answer it?" Spiderelli asked.

"N-no," said Maggie, and at once she began racking her brain for a suitable lie. Under no circumstances should she tell this stranger anything more than he had already guessed.

"Might be important," he said when the phone rang again.

"It's—we're on a party line," Maggie said finally. "That's the ring for the other house."

"What other house? This side of the island looks like darkest Africa." When the phone rang once more he asked, "You really aren't going to pick that up?"

"No," Maggie said doggedly. "It's not for me."

"Maybe you ought to take a message for your neighbor, at least? Here, it's—"

"Don't touch that!"

He had stood up and was reaching for the receiver, but the sharpness of Maggie's voice stopped him cold. Curious, Spiderelli looked at Maggie and waited.

Tense and scared, she insisted, "It's the neighbor's line. Just leave it alone. I don't want—just don't bother with it."

"The message might be important."

"So is respecting their privacy. Just *leave* it, damn you!"

The issue was settled when the phone silenced itself. Maggie turned around and pretended to be busy at the sink. She turned on the water full blast.

After a moment Spiderelli asked, "You want to tell me what's going on?"

"Nothing," Maggie replied. "Nothing whatever."

He circled the counter. "Look, Amy Vanderbilt didn't cuss at the drop of the hat. It doesn't take a genius to see that you're upset." He shut off the faucet with a jerk. Standing slightly behind her, he asked, "You got some kind of problem?"

A problem? Oh, yes, definitely a problem, all right, but Maggie wasn't about to spill the story to anyone, let alone this character.

"The only thing that's wrong," Maggie replied composedly, willing herself not to sidle away from him, "is that I was interrupted during my work."

He leaned one elbow on the counter and smiled, not the least bit insulted. "You referring to me?"

"Precisely," said Maggie. She reached for a hand towel and used it briskly. "If you don't mind, Mr. Spiderelli, I'm afraid I must ask you to leave. I'm very busy, you see, and—"

"I get the idea," he said. Unruffled, he strolled around the counter again and headed for the doorway, beer in hand. "You like your privacy and I've invaded long enough. You don't have to ask twice. On the other hand," he said, turning back and framing himself in the doorway, "maybe you ought to know that trouble is my business. I'm considered a useful kind of guy when the chips are down."

She'd just bet he was. He didn't develop a body like that singing in the church choir. "No, thanks," she said. "I'm sure I can take care of any trouble that comes along."

Unless it was already there.

That thought sent a shot of adrenaline through Maggie's entire body. Standing in the warm and sunny kitchen, looking at Mick Spiderelli as he grinned lazily down at her, Maggie was suddenly filled with horror, the kind of fear that starts out big and scary and gets bigger and more frightening with every heartbeat. Like murky black floodwaters, the horror began to boil and gush inside her.

"My God," she said, and put one hand to her mouth.

It would be just Ben's style to hire someone to do his dirty work. All along Maggie had expected Ben to come alone. He had vowed to find Elizabeth, and until that moment Maggie hadn't anticipated that he might have paid someone else to actually follow through on the threat. *Could* he have sent this man? *Of course,* she nearly cried out. Yes! How like Ben to overreact and hire a Mafia-style executioner to locate a five-year-old!

"Dear heaven," said Maggie as she pushed past him. Running up the stairs and across the cool stone floor of the corridor, she shouted, *"Elizabeth!"*

Two

But Elizabeth wasn't on the beach. Nor was she playing in the salon or sunning on the terrace. She had disappeared. The surf crashed upon the empty sand and a quickening breeze carried no childish cries or laughing chatter. The beautiful setting suddenly looked as barren as a desert and frighteningly foreign. Maggie panicked.

"Elizabeth!"

Not thinking, not even breathing if that was possible, Maggie fled down the zigzag and raced headlong onto the empty beach. *"Elizabeth!"*

Mick Spiderelli swooped down the path after her. "Hey," he shouted.

Maggie turned like a cornered fox before a pack of hounds. "Don't," she commanded, holding out both hands as if they might be capable of stopping him.

Too late, Maggie realized she hadn't managed to make her voice audible. She had barely mustered a croak. He didn't stop but kept coming and looked as if he was going to make a grab for her. When he was just a step away from seizing her, Maggie gathered all her strength and smacked him across the face. Hard.

"Damn you!" she cried. "What have you done with my child?"

Big as he was, Mick Spiderelli reeled from the blow, put his hand to his cheek and shifted to regain his balance. He blinked and stared. Nothing had prepared him for staid Yankee Dear Miss Margaret slapping him like a fishwife. "Take it easy," he said, wide-eyed. "I haven't done anything!"

"Where is she?" Maggie demanded, following him until they were practically nose to nose. No longer afraid, Maggie felt angry instead. "You've got an accomplice, haven't you? I was so stupid! Is she out on your boat? Is that it?"

He didn't answer—not immediately, at least, and Maggie didn't have any time to waste. She whirled away and ran clumsily across the sand, gathering speed as she reached the water's edge. She tore off her shirt and flung it onto the beach, prepared to swim to the ends of the earth if she had to. Spiderelli caught up with her just as she splashed into the ocean.

"Wait," he said, and seized her elbow.

Maggie tried to shake him off and swing another blow at him, but he was ready this time and ducked. He spun her away from him without letting go, and they wrestled for an instant. Maggie sloshed in the foamy water to regain her footing. Instinctively she clawed and kicked, but he seemed to know just which way to fend off each attack.

"Stop," he ordered, holding Maggie just out of striking range as easily as if she'd been dancing with him.

Half crying, half panting, Maggie shrieked an unintelligible curse at him. "You were tricking me!" Fighting to get free in a frenzy of flying water and windblown hair, she cried, "You've stolen her!"

"Simmer down! Talk some sense, will you?"

"How much did he pay you?" she demanded, breathless from the struggle. "I'll make it more, I promise! I can get as much as you want! Just, please, please, let her go. Don't take her away."

"For crying out loud, I was sitting with you having a beer and—*ouch*—dammit! That *hurts*! They've walked off down the beach, that's all. Stop it!"

"She wouldn't do that. Elizabeth would never wander off!"

"Never say never where kids are concerned. Look—"

"Let me *go*!"

He obeyed finally—perhaps out of self-defense—and Maggie didn't stand around and argue. At once, she wheeled around and plunged into the ocean. She leaped over an incoming crest, another and another, until she was thigh-deep. Then she dived into the water. She'd always been a good swimmer, and now she struck out for the boat, with long, powerful strokes.

"It's a waste of time," Spiderelli shouted at her through cupped hands.

Maggie barely heard him. His words didn't even register. She swam directly toward the smaller of the two boats anchored nearly a hundred yards from shore, not even allowing for the tide and current. The natural forces in the bay pushed her off course, and she had to backtrack until finally she trod water breathlessly beside the hull.

"Elizabeth!" she shouted, hardly able to raise her voice for lack of oxygen. Her breath came in huge, sucking gasps. "Elizabeth, answer me!"

When she heard no response, Maggie breaststroked around the boat and found a ladder. She climbed up, hand over hand, and landed on a postage stamp-size deck. The boat's topside had been thoroughly cleared of any gear except for a fishing rod that was propped against the rail and a pair of worn-out men's sneakers abandoned as if they'd been kicked off before he dived over the side for a swim. There were no signs of any children.

Dripping saltwater and still breathing like a spent marathon runner, Maggie hurried to the cabin hatch and let herself down the two-step ladder. "Elizabeth?"

The main cabin looked like the interior of a camping trailer, complete with a small refrigerator, propane stove and pull-down table with cushioned bench. A glance told Maggie that the occupants of the boat were neither wealthy nor interested in the trappings money could buy. The furnishings were worn but clean, the floorboards had been recently painted but not carpeted and the simple smell of fried fish hung in the humid air. A net bag of apples and oranges swayed from its peg on the wall. Tacked up on a cheap bulletin board over the sink was a calendar advertising a bait and tackle shop and picturing a leaping swordfish, with the days of the month carefully crossed off. Not a cup or pencil was out of place, and yet the boat conveyed a distinctly homey feeling. A photograph of Spider in his father's baseball cap grinned down from the bulletin board, and the sight of it actually hurt Maggie. Her own child had never felt so far away.

No signs of a struggle showed, thank heaven. To make absolutely sure Elizabeth hadn't been brought aboard, Maggie shoved open two other doors and found a very small bathroom and another cabin for sleeping in. Clothes hung from hooks, and a neat rack of paperback books, including a series of Berenstein Bears titles, had been built in over the porthole. Even the bed had been made. There were no clues to Elizabeth's disappearance.

With a cry of frustration, Maggie charged back up on deck.

Mick flung himself over the rail of the boat, dripping and out of breath and blocking her path like a huge, hulking linebacker. Maggie rushed past him, ready to dive into the water again, but Mick grabbed her arm and Maggie cried, "Let me go!"

He panted, wrestling with her. "I'm beginning to think you're not as smart as you look, Miss Margaret. Where the hell are you going now?"

"Out to that other boat. Let me *go*!"

But he held her tight. "Think," he ordered. "Drowning isn't going to do anyone any good."

"I've got to find her!"

"The kids have to be around here somewhere. They just wandered off for a minute, that's all. Don't panic. My kid's missing, too, but you don't see me going crazy. It's counterproductive."

"You don't understand! She's everything in my life. My daughter is *everything*!"

His black eyes bore into hers, and his face was rock-still for an instant. Maggie held her breath, suddenly more frightened than ever before by the animal fierceness she felt in his grip, the look in his eye. But abruptly Mick released her and stepped back without a word.

Maggie took the chance. She dived off the boat into the surging blue-green water and began to swim. Mick did not give chase. Against the tide once more, Maggie struck out for the other boat, the larger yacht lying farther out in the bay.

Halfway there, she could hardly keep going. The bay had turned choppy, and the powerful, almost insidious underwater pull of the tide prevented her from reaching the yacht. A sound like static roared in her ears, a fire burned in her lungs. There was no fighting it.

Nearly weeping with fury at her own weakness, Maggie stopped swimming. A wave slapped her face and she choked. Her arms felt like lead, her legs were numb from exertion. Too frightened to think, she'd pushed herself beyond her limit and it hadn't worked. The sea tugged at her body as if she were a helpless leaf. The tide pulled inexorably.

Elizabeth lost? At the thought, Maggie experienced a gut-quickening sensation akin to déjà vu. She nearly retched. She was living her nightmare, the awful dream that had begun the morning of Elizabeth's birth. Her baby stolen? How many times had she been awakened by the thought? The horror? Being parted from her daughter had plagued Maggie with the regularity that only a single parent could know. Five years of watchfulness, of agonizing each time the child wandered out of her sight, of finding joy in even the smallest or most irritating moments together—could it end as abruptly as this? Was the life she had created for them over?

"No," Maggie moaned. She wasn't too exhausted to feel desperation. The panic closed in as swiftly as the tide had done—squeezing, chilling, wrenching her heart. Feebly, Maggie cast her face up to the sky. "Please," she prayed, "help me now."

Another wave closed over her head, forced Maggie down. Down and down. Miraculously, though, her plea was answered. A strong arm swept around Maggie's shoulders and pulled her back to life. He supported her there, one hand cupped at the nape of her neck to hold her above the waves, the other steadying the both of them in the water. Lithe and strong as a dolphin, Mick Spiderelli kicked and bobbed next to Maggie. His hair was slick, but he was barely out of breath. "Come on," he said. "Get into the dingy."

He had been smarter than she. An inflatable rubber boat bobbed a few yards away, and Mick towed her toward it. Maggie felt weaker than the proverbial kitten, and she couldn't climb in. Mick boosted her over the side, and she sprawled in the bow of the ungainly little boat. She lay there, struggling to breathe and not cry. Mick surged out of the water and into the dingy beside her.

He didn't speak, but settled himself at the oars. He was strong and quickly found a swift rhythm that propelled them toward the yacht in a straight line. Having set a course of action, Mick was executing it without wasting time. She should have had the sense to do the same. When Mick rowed within hailing distance of the yacht, Maggie sat up.

"Hey there!" he shouted, shipping his lightweight oars and allowing the dingy to drift. "Anybody there?"

A head popped up from the behind the railing of the moored yacht. "Ahoy!" came the answering shout.

The yacht was long and elegant, a beautiful fairy-tale boat that would dance before a playful breeze and race for the open sea if the wind changed to her liking. Her hull shimmered as the ocean lapped at her curving sides, and her rigging whispered softly, as if she had life of her own. Tugging gently at her anchoring line, she looked anxious to escape the captivity of the small bay. The words Diana My Love, Boca Raton were painted on her stern.

An expensive network of canary-yellow-canvas skirting had been lashed to the boat's railing. The head that had appeared there rose higher and turned into a dapper elderly gentleman. He pulled a pipe from his teeth, his expression understandably startled at finding a cheap rubber dingy bumping his beautiful boat.

Sounding as amiable as a neighbor talking over a picket fence, Mick said, "Say, have you seen a couple of kids around here lately?"

The gentleman who got up from one of the lounge chairs wore a yachting cap, white trousers and a pink polo shirt with an ascot. He had been smoking a pipe, and he knocked it—by habit, no doubt—against the railing. "Kids?" he said, willing to jest with these strange passersby. "You think they rode their bicycles out here or something?"

Smiling, Mick shook his head. "No, they just wandered away. We're afraid—well, we thought they might have tried to con their way aboard your boat."

"Trick-or-treating, are they?" joshed the pink-shirted gentleman. He leaned his elbows on the railing and smiled down at them. "No, I haven't seen 'em, but you're welcome to come aboard if you want to make sure."

Instinct told Maggie there was nothing to fear from this polite fellow, but she didn't trust her intuition much at that moment. Though the invitation to come aboard had been merely a civility, Maggie clambered up a stainless-steel ladder and arrived on the polished wooden deck of the *Diana*.

"I'm sorry to intrude," she said quickly, "but I'm terribly worried."

The gentleman had kind blue eyes, and he seemed to guess her state of mind exactly. "Have a look," he invited, gesturing with his pipe to indicate the entire yacht. "I'll just chat with your husband here. What kind of dingy is that, young man?"

Maggie didn't pause to hear the answer or to set the man straight about her marital status. She simply made a beeline for the cabin door and let herself into a beautifully appointed saloon.

The *Diana* compared most favorably to Mick Spiderelli's smaller craft. His boat looked definitely like that of a poor man, while *Diana* had clearly cost her owner twenty times what Mick Spiderelli had paid. There were even servants aboard. Maggie surprised a chef and a white-coated steward in the galley and the boat's captain and his mate up on the forward deck. But no children.

Freshly frightened and visibly trembling, Maggie returned to the lounge deck.

Mick hadn't moved from his seat in the dingy, but he had obviously spent the past few minutes chatting with their host. When Maggie appeared, his dark eyes glinted and he said, "Back already, darling? This is Peter Samson."

"Hello," said Maggie, automatically shaking the older man's proffered hand.

He clasped her hand gently. "Nice to meet you, Mrs. Spiderelli. Don't worry about those youngsters. I was watching them on the beach just ten minutes ago. Having a wonderful time they were, too. Playing pirates, if my guess is correct. I'll bet you'll find them hiding up in those rocks. See?"

Maggie looked up on the hillside where Mr. Samson pointed, and she peered along a scrag of rocks with her eyes shielded. "Have you a pair of binoculars?" she asked.

"Certainly."

A moment later Peter Samson pressed a pair of glasses into her hands. Maggie used them to carefully scan the hillside. Once she thought she saw a flash of movement, but she backtracked and couldn't find it again. Still, she was fairly certain she had seen something. Hurriedly she returned the binoculars to Mr. Samson. "Thank you," she said in a rush, anxious to get to those rocks. "If you see them soon, will you—"

"I'll certainly alert you, Mrs. Spiderelli," Mr. Samson assured her. "With the storm coming up, I'm sure you'll want to have them safely tucked under your wing."

"Storm?" said Maggie, pausing at the railing to turn and stare at him. She shot a look up at the sky and was startled to see a boiling bank of iron-gray clouds scudding in from the horizon.

"Dear heaven," she said.

"I'm sorry," said Peter Samson. "I've frightened you again. I just—"

Mick saw the look of terror cross her face. If it was possible, Margaret Kincaid paled to an even lighter color than before.

"That's torn it," Mick said from the dingy, trying to sound laconic. "Come on, love." He shook his head and said to Samson, "I try not to tell her about bad weather until it actually hits. These Yankee Thoroughbreds are nervous types, you know."

Peter Samson laughed. "I know what you mean. My wife, Diana, had a pedigree back to the *Mayflower*. How'd those people make it across the ocean without a healthy attitude toward foul weather?"

"Beats me," said Mick. "My relatives were so far down in steerage all they knew about storms came by rumor."

Samson chuckled. "Well, take my advice, my boy. I used to ply Diana with sherry before a nor'easter. It always saw her through. More fun for me that way, too." And he winked broadly at Mick.

Mick laughed. "We'll have to try that."

He reached to help the Kincaid woman down into the dingy, and she reluctantly accepted his assistance, not meeting his eye. Unspeaking, she slid into a spot as far from Mick as she could get.

"So long," he said, and cast off. Using one of the oars, he paddled a safe distance from the yacht before putting both oars into their locks and getting to the business of rowing them back to shore. Peter Samson waved jauntily as they drew away.

When he had rowed them out of earshot, Maggie said, "You son of a bitch."

"Listen," Mick said, unruffled by her tone. "I'm helping you, aren't I?"

"I'm not so sure. At least you could have told him we weren't married."

"I figured I ought to make polite conversation, you know? I mean, you were going through his boat like you were the SS or something. The least I could do was—"

"She's my daughter, damn you!"

In spite of her previous efforts to hold it all together, Maggie's voice cracked and wavered. At once, she pressed both her hands against her mouth and shut her eyes. Sure enough, a second later a tear stole out from under one of her lashes. Quickly, she turned her face away.

Even the world's biggest heel would have been affected by the sight of that pretty, pale woman shivering in her too-sexy bathing suit and struggling to hold on to her composure.

After a moment, Mick said, "Take it easy. We'll find your daughter."

She didn't react, and that was all either of them said until the dingy scraped bottom on the beach. Mick rowed and she shut up. When foamy breakers boiled against the sides of the rubber boat, Margaret Kincaid apparently couldn't get away from him soon enough. She jumped out of the dingy, landing thigh-deep in rushing water that nearly swept her down. The surf was strong, and the wind snatched at the dark cloud of her hair. She grabbed the bow of the dingy to save herself from falling.

Mick jumped out of the dingy and finished the job of dragging the little boat well up out of the water. When they reached dry sand, he dropped the boat and glanced unconsciously at the sky.

A storm was definitely on its way. Maggie looked up, too.

"Don't panic," said Mick, understanding her silence. "The bad weather's not here yet."

She looked directly at him. Her voice sounded surprisingly strong. "How bad is it supposed to get?"

He didn't lie. "Bad," he said. "A hurricane, in fact."

"A *hurricane*?"

Mick found his Mets' cap where he'd thrown it onto the sand. He picked it up, slapped it against his leg and looked at her. "Yeah, a hurricane. You ever listen to the radio?"

"It's in the servants' room," she replied defensively. "I let them have a day off, and I didn't bother—"

"Well, a hell of a rainstorm's on its way," Mick interrupted, not caring to hear the details about her domestic help. They had bigger problems on the way. "A storm pounded most of New Jersey into a swamp yesterday, and they're closing parts of the Carolina coast to all traffic because storms are building all over the place. That's why I put in here. I'm not riding out a hurricane on the high seas."

She was quiet. Then, in a whisper that was nearly blown away on the wind, she said, "We've got to find them."

"Yes," said Mick. There was definitely no time to waste. "Tell me a few things. Is there a restaurant or resort or something near by? They might have decided to—"

"There's nothing at this end of the island. Elizabeth knows that."

"All right. Could they have gone into the house? Maybe they're in a bathroom or found a way to the wine cellar or—"

She shook her head. "We'd have heard them or seen them."

"You're sure?"

"Yes, the kitchen is located so that all the rooms are within speaking distance."

"Never far from the butler, is that it?"

Stung, she began, "Look—"

"Never mind," said Mick roughly. He stared down the beach, frowning. Spider had a habit of disappearing at the most inconvenient times, and he'd certainly picked the worst day to do it this time around. "All right, if they're not in the house, we'll look out here. The rocks, you think?"

"That's what your friend Samson said."

He didn't acknowledge her sarcastic tone. "Okay, you try jogging down the beach, then, and I'll climb up and have a look—"

Maggie gathered her courage and faced Mick Spiderelli. "No," she said.

He half turned to look down at her. "What?"

Determined to stand up to him no matter how scary he seemed, Maggie said, "I—we'll have to stick together."

He began to smile, but it wasn't the amused grin he'd used before. There was no sparkle in his black eyes this time. His expression was cold. "Don't trust me, do you?"

"No," she said.

He shrugged. "At least you're honest. Okay, let's go. The longer we argue—"

"This way," said Maggie, already on the move.

She led him up the zigzag again as far as the first turn. Using her arms to part the thick swath of day lilies that grew along the stone wall, Maggie started toward it. The wall was just a few inches too high, that was all. Without waiting to be asked, Mick grasped her bare ankle and boosted Maggie up and into a flowerbed. She scrambled ahead of him, stepping carefully through the flowers and swishing the tall grasses aside. Ahead of her, the hillside looked like an overgrown jungle, all right. Moss covered the ground, moisture-laden tropical plants waved eerily in the breeze and hunks of creepy dead leaves swayed from tree branches.

As easily as a mountain lion, Mick sprang after her and ducked under the low-hanging bough of a tree. "Oh, boy," he said. "I knew I should have packed my elephant gun."

In the lead, Maggie pushed past waist-deep plants and called, "Elizabeth!"

Much louder, Mick bellowed, *"Spider!"*

"Ridiculous name," Maggie muttered, then lifted her head and shouted, "Elizabeth!"

"At least he's not a ridiculous kid," Mick growled, making steady but very loud progress in the thick undergrowth behind her. *"Spider!"*

"Are you suggesting there's something wrong with my daughter?"

"Nothing that a week of making mud pies wouldn't cure."

Maggie plowed through a tangle of brambles, not caring if a thorny branch snapped back and whacked him in the face. "My daughter is a well-bred young lady."

"Sure, with all the fun squished out of her. *Spider!*"

Maggie spun around, panting hard. "Elizabeth is a very fun-loving child. She's just fine."

"Right," Mick shot back. "That's why she disobeyed you and ran off with the first red-blooded kid who came down the beach. Open your eyes, Miss Margaret. Every kid needs to cut loose once in a while."

"I suppose you think you're an expert on child-rearing?"

"I'm no amateur," he retorted.

"You're a thug!"

He didn't miss a beat, ready to match her insult for insult. "*You're* a prissy old woman."

"I'm not old!"

"You *act* like an eighty-year-old dowager."

Maggie let go of the leafy frond she'd been holding, and it swatted Mick smack across his cheek. Red-hot, Maggie set off up the steep slope once more, shouting, "Elizabeth! Come down here at once! *Elizabeth!*"

She should have been more careful of where she was going. And, of course, taking two minutes to put on a pair of shoes would have helped immensely. But Maggie was boiling mad as well as scared stiff. She stepped on a sharp rock, then a thorn jabbed her in the thigh and finally something slithery moved under her bare foot. She squealed, then cursed herself at once for acting like such a ninny. One little snake wasn't going to come between her and the most important person in her life! But the little snake turned out to have brothers and sisters—a dozen at least—and before she could stop herself, Maggie was screaming.

Mick caught her in his arms from behind just as she started to lose control. Neatly, he spun around and deposited her in the weeds behind him. Then he turned back to do battle with the snakes.

"It's just a little nest," he said over his shoulder. "And they're not poisonous. You don't have to go berserk."

"I'm not berserk." Maggie hugged herself to hold in the heebie-jeebies. "I'm—I was just startled, that's all. I wasn't scared."

"Right," Mick said, sounding as if he wasn't going to believe her any farther than he could throw her. He stood back from the writhing mass of baby snakes and glanced at her to make sure she hadn't fainted. Grimly, he noted that she was still upright, and nodded. "I'll lead from now on."

Maggie longed to argue. Oh, she wished she could! But Mick didn't wait for an answer, and his progress up the junglelike hill was infinitely more steady than hers had been. She skirted the nest of snakes and climbed after him through the increasingly thick undergrowth. The mosquitoes ignored Mick completely and attacked Maggie with a vengeance. She swatted at them as they stung her bare skin.

One bush after another revealed no children hiding in play. Nor could Maggie hear the giggles and cries Elizabeth usually made when engaged in some let's-pretend fantasy game. In addition to the wet slick of seawater still clinging to her in the humid air, Maggie felt sweat spring out on her skin.

A clammy minute or two later, Mick gave a crow of triumph. "Look!"

He reached into a leafy thicket and came up with a wet and soiled bit of fabric.

Maggie cried out. "That's Elizabeth's bathing suit!"

"It means we're on the right trail, at least," said Mick, squinting up the slope. Above them lay the first tumble of rocks, and he scanned them for signs of the children.

Maggie snatched the bathing suit out of his grasp. "It means that horrible little boy of yours is encouraging my daughter to—to—"

"Quit jabbering. Let's go."

Mick heaved his frame over the first outcrop of huge boulders. He turned and extended his hand down to Maggie. "Relax," he said, grinning. "Spider hasn't passed his first year of medical school yet."

With a glower at him, Maggie allowed Mick to pull her up onto the boulders. From that vantage point they could see down a long stretch of cascading rocks. If the forest had looked like Eden grown rampant, then this spot had been the site of a terrible battle between God and his demonic enemies. Huge stones looked as though they'd been flung to earth from a distant mountaintop, and reedy stalks of tall grass grew determinedly out of the smallest squares of soil.

"Elizabeth!" Maggie called.

At long last they heard an answering shout. Not very strong, and most of it snatched away on the wind.

Mick cupped his hands. *"Spider!"*

The boy's small head appeared over the weedy tufts growing on the rocks below. His expression wasn't cocky or devilish at all this time. In an instant Maggie saw that the boy was frightened.

"Daddy!" he called.

Mick said "Come on" to Maggie and reached to help her down the first rocks.

"Go on ahead," Maggie said, her heart in her throat, knowing she would only slow him down. "I can catch up."

He did as he was told and leaped agilely from one boulder to the next. He reached Spider's location in seconds and disappeared into the rocks.

Maggie arrived a minute later, out of breath and more frightened than ever before. "She's all right?" she cried.

Mick lifted his head. His face was set, as if he knew he'd better put on a good front. "She's okay," he said, sounding almost too normal. "But she's stuck," he added. "Be careful where you step. She's wedged back inside the rocks."

Maggie flung herself down on the rough stones beside him. It wasn't a cave exactly, but more of a ledge—two large boulders supported by a rubble of smaller stones. How any child could have crawled inside was inexplicable to Maggie. "Hurry," she said. "The storm will be here any minute. Let me—"

"No! Take it easy." Mick put both arms out to block Maggie and stopped her short. "Just slow down," he commanded, holding her fast in a grip that hurt. "This operation is going to take some time."

"Why? Please, just hurry—"

She nearly succeeded in slipping out of his grip, and he seized her shoulders hard, pinching her into a standstill. "Stop," he said. "The rocks are unstable. The whole thing could cave in on her any second."

Three

———

Terrified, Maggie crouched forward on hands and knees. A dark gap hardly big enough for a spaniel to stand up in lay between two shards of split boulder, and she could just make out a small bare foot inside. "Elizabeth?"

A tiny sob came from the darkened cave. "Mama?"

"Yes, it's me, darling. Just stay still, honey. We'll have you out in a jiffy."

"She can't get out," Spider said without a shred of tact. "We were pirates, see, and went inside to hide the treasure, but something moved. She's really *stuck*."

"Steady," said Mick, and Maggie realized she had sobbed.

He put his hand on the back of her neck and squeezed once, then released her and crouched forward to get a better look at the rocks that entombed the child. "We'll just take a minute to look over the situation," he said gently. "Elizabeth? Can you hear me?"

"I—I can hear" came the small-voiced reply. "I can see you, too."

"Atta girl," said Mick, peeking into the cave. "We're going to need your help, okay? Can you tell me what's stuck?"

"My arm," she said.

"Does it hurt?"

Elizabeth thought that over before replying. "No," she said. "It's just stuck."

"Gotcha," said Mick. "You think I can get in there with you? Can you slide yourself over?"

"You're pretty big," Elizabeth said doubtfully.

"We'll see," said Mick, and he twisted around to lie flat on his back. He felt his way along the broken ceiling of the entrance first, then used his legs to push his way inside. His bare back scraped the sandy rock, and Maggie gasped involuntarily. The stone must have hurt like hell.

Spider looked at her, guessing her thought. "It's okay," he said with confidence. "My dad's tough."

Just then Mick swore horribly.

He had disappeared up to his waist, using both upper-body strength and leverage from his feet to inch his way inside. Maggie couldn't imagine what he might have seen or encountered in the darkness. Anxiously, she hunched forward. "What's wrong?"

He muttered another oath and growled, "I just bumped my nose."

Elizabeth giggled.

"You laughing at me, kid?" he demanded, wrestling his way closer to the trapped child.

"Yes," said Elizabeth. "You're funny."

"So I've been told," he muttered. "A million laughs. Let's see the arm."

"Here," said Elizabeth, sounding as if she had no qualms about trusting him. Maggie wished it was she who could comfort her child instead of a hulking stranger, but she had to be content with listening to what transpired inside the cave.

"Hmm," murmured Mick.

"Well?" asked Maggie when she could stand no more.

Mick was silent a little longer.

"Well?"

"Your mom's the impatient type, isn't she?"

"What's impatient?" Elizabeth asked.

"She wants everything right away."

"For heaven's sake!" Maggie burst out. "What's going on?"

"Well," said Mick, sounding calm, "I think we can get her out. There's just one rock pinning her, and it's not too big. I can hold it, but I can't untangle her, too. Can you squish in here, too?"

"Me?" asked Maggie, startled by the idea. "You mean with you?"

She shouldn't have hesitated. The chance to get in there with Elizabeth should have tempted her at once. But knowing that Elizabeth was essentially safe for the moment gave Maggie a second to think clearly. After all, the cave was hardly big enough for Mick to fit by himself. Crawling in there with him did not appeal to Maggie in the least. The fact that Mick Spiderelli's lower body was the only part of him that lay exposed to her view made Maggie's hesitation even longer. He had cocked one long leg up, and the other was stretched out as if he had lain down to bathe in the sunshine. Muscle and bone combined in a supreme male display. His worn cutoff shorts did little to disguise the lean tautness of his hips and outlined the most male part of his anatomy—even in repose—for all the world to see. He was a sexy man, for heaven's sake, and even at the moment when Maggie's whole being should have been consumed by getting Elizabeth out of the wretched spot, she couldn't help

acknowledging that the idea of sliding into the small confines of the cave with him shocked her. Not a little. A lot.

"Come on," said Mick, totally unaware of her fleeting
dilemma. "We'd better try."

Maggie thanked her stars he couldn't see her blushing.
"I—I don't think—"

"She's too big," said Spider. "She's got a big chest."

Mick began to laugh in spite of the gravity of the moment, and Maggie clamped down on a fresh surge of humiliated frustration.

Mystified, Spider asked, "What'd I say?"

"Never mind. All right, Spider," Mick agreed. "Wiggle
up here, can you? And Miss Margaret?"

"Yes?" Maggie said, already helping the eager Spider to
crawl in past his father's legs.

"See if you can find a rock big enough to fit the entrance, will you? I'd like some assurance this whole thing
won't come crashing down. No—wait!" This as Spider
nearly reached his father's chest. The boy froze.

"What is it?" Maggie cried.

"Ouch," said Elizabeth.

"Spider, hold this," Mick ordered.

"I can't reach. It's—"

"Here!" said Mick, urgent as before.

"Ouch," Elizabeth insisted.

"Dear God!" Fists clenched, Maggie raged, "I feel so
helpless!" Desperately, she fell upon a stump of a tree en-
crusted with sand and crawling with ants. With strength
fueled by fear, she wrestled it closer to the ledge.

"Ouch!" Elizabeth cried.

Spider bellowed, *"Ow!"*

And the rock shifted. The giant slab of stone gave a groan
and moved.

"Go!" yelled Mick.

Spider scrambled out quick as a mouse, and right behind him came Elizabeth, scuttling like a crab on her back. Dirt and tears had smeared paths down her cheeks and her blue-gray eyes were wide and terrified, but she was alive and Maggie grabbed her. There was no time for a hug. Maggie pushed both children aside and dived for the cave, trying her damnedest to shove the stump into place to keep the rock from crushing Mick entirely. She braced herself and pushed with both hands.

"Hurry!" she gasped.

"Son of a—"

"Quick, it's going!"

"Now *I'm* stuck!"

"Dear lord," Maggie cried. The stump gave way and rolled perfectly into place. And before she realized what she was doing, Maggie wriggled down beside it and lay on her side, trying valiantly to shove the rubble of smaller stones out of the way. By the merest shaft of light she realized Mick had caught his head between the slabs of rock. Not only that, but he had managed to keep the cave from falling in by bracing his elbows on the floor and holding the rock up himself. The stump had saved him from a slow, crushing death, but still trapped, he lay there and swore.

Breathless, Maggie said, "Watch your language. Remember the children."

"They sure as hell better remember me," he said, panting, "when I'm dead and gone!"

"If you keep talking like that, they'll never forget."

"Miss Margaret," he said, his voice distorted by the physical effort of keeping his neck twisted to one side, "did anyone ever tell you what you ought to do with your good manners?"

"Be quiet," she ordered. "You'll use up all the oxygen or something."

He laughed, but caught his breath and stopped abruptly.

Maggie slid higher next to him and dug at the bits of stone and sand that imprisoned him. "There. Now bring your head toward me and—"

"Got it," said Mick.

They worked in unison, first Maggie taking hold of the rock above them, then Mick sliding closer and getting his head free. They bumped foreheads, but in a flurry of quick, sweating moves that included plenty of negotiating arms and legs, they were both out in the daylight and breathing as if they'd run for miles along the beach.

"Whew," said Mick, a grin on his face as he wiped the worst of the sand and dust away from his eyes. "Anyone ever tell you how good you are in a pinch, Miss Margaret?"

"There wasn't room for a pinch in there," she retorted, reaching for her naked but safe daughter. Hugging Elizabeth for all she was worth, Maggie added without thinking, "And my name's not Miss Margaret. It's Maggie."

Mick laughed, the man who had given her her daughter back actually *laughed* as carelessly as if he'd just played a few innings of baseball. Maggie closed her eyes and wondered if she'd ever take life so lightly. She squeezed Elizabeth until the little girl giggled and wiggled like a pup. "Mama, I'm *okay*," she said.

Spider said, "It's raining, y'know."

He was right. The stiff wind had begun to spit a sharp and very cold rain that hit Maggie's skin like the pricking of needles. Elizabeth shivered.

"Here," said Maggie, trying to be brusque and parental. "Get your suit on, miss. You're never to take it off, do you understand me? Let's get back to the house."

Elizabeth obeyed, and Maggie caught an amused glance that passed between Mick and his son. Amusement, yes, but also something else was communicated in the vivid look between father and son. Thanks and love were conveyed in a single, mischievous glance.

"C'mon," said Mick, elbowing his son. "Let's whistle up Silver and ride out of here, Tonto."

"Huh?" said Spider.

"No, please," Maggie intervened, assisting Elizabeth with the straps to her bathing suit. "You can't disappear like the Lone Ranger. Come with us. The storm is coming down around our ears and you might as well—I mean—the least we can do is—"

"I got the impression," Mick said mildly, still sitting on the rocks, "that you thought I had something to do with your daughter's disappearance."

Mercifully unflustered, Maggie said hastily, "I must have been wrong. Please. Come down to the house. It will certainly be safer than sitting out the storm on your boat."

He tilted his head and grinned at her, looking far from saviorlike. "Maybe not."

They scrambled down the hillside with the rain pelting down around them. Once inside the villa, Maggie pulled the French doors closed and the four of them turned around to watch as the storm descended with all the sound and fury of a true hurricane.

"Your boat," said Maggie.

Mick shrugged. "It's as well protected as I can make it." A jagged crack of lightning tore across the sky, and he added, "You'd better load your cannon if you hope to chase me out there."

"I don't think," said Maggie, "that you'd be intimidated by one little cannon."

He grinned. "Probably right."

Maggie sent the children directly to the bathtub. She ran it full of steaming hot water and bubble bath and left the two of them cavorting.

"Coeducational bathing," remarked Mick, one eyebrow raised as he lingered in the doorway indulgently. "Isn't that too risqué for your sensitive daughter?"

Maggie sent him a cool look that told him to shut up. "How about a shower for you?" she asked, opening the door to the adjacent guest bathroom and gesturing him inside. "Plenty of hot water and I'll unpack the bandages afterward."

Reminded of his injuries, Mick checked his appearance in the mirror. His face had been scraped in a few places, and patches of his back had been rubbed raw and looked very sore. When he touched one spot, he even winced. Warily, he glanced at Maggie. "Are you a sadist with Merthiolate?"

"No," said Maggie with the beginning of a smile. "But if you're worried, you can have a drink to numb the pain."

"A shower and a beer," he said, and sighed. "I've died and gone to heaven."

Shaking her head, Maggie closed the door and left him alone. A few minutes later she heard the water start to run in the bathroom, and Mick began to sing. His Elvis Presley imitation wasn't bad. Maggie found herself smiling as she headed for her own bath.

She took a fast shower herself—with very hot water and unperfumed soap—in the bath connected to the master suite. She told herself she ought to relax now that the crisis was over, but she couldn't quite. As the wind battered the shutters outside her room, she dressed in a simple, stretchy jumpsuit, an outfit that felt marvelously warm and cuddly after her afternoon's excitement. A pair of flat-heeled white sandals made her feel sufficiently dressed to entertain even a hit man and his son for dinner. Looking at her reflection in the still-steamy bathroom mirror, however, Maggie decided not to make up her face. Lipstick and mascara might give her houseguest the wrong impression. She suspected that if Mick Spiderelli took it in his head to have something—even a woman—he'd stop at nothing until he got what he wanted. Therefore—no makeup, no jewelry, no perfume. Maggie brushed her hair, pinned it primly up again and went to check on the children.

Elizabeth and Spider were still happily playing in the tub, so Maggie left them to their fun for a while longer. In the kitchen she prepared a pot of hot chocolate, opened a bottle of beer and took the drinks on a tray toward the bedroom wing. Along the way she stopped at the sideboard and poured herself a portion of Scotch from a crystal decanter. Normally, she didn't care for hard liquor, but some situations called for it. Outside, the wind and rain battered the house, and when her hands shook as she replaced the stopper on the decanter, Maggie wondered if a sister storm hadn't managed to find its way inside herself. Hail stones pelted the skylight, and every rattle felt as if it pierced her skin and stung her nerve endings.

She'd been careless with Elizabeth. She could never let it happen again. Ever.

A gleeful shout from the bedrooms stirred Maggie from her troubled state and told her that the children had gotten out of the bath. Hurriedly, Maggie pulled herself together. After another fortifying sip of Scotch, she carried the tray of drinks to the bedroom wing, hoping she looked like a composed hostess.

The children must have had some assistance from Mick, because they were dressed. Elizabeth wore her nightgown, and Spider had been persuaded to put on her bathrobe—a powder-blue quilted number which he tied with a cowboy belt instead of the usual bit of lacy material Elizabeth used. He was receiving a formal tour of Elizabeth's toys, particularly Kangaroy, a much beloved stuffed kangaroo. Maggie left the cups of hot chocolate on the dresser and didn't interrupt.

Mick had left all the connecting doors open, and Maggie found him wearing a thankfully large towel around his hips and lounging, with long legs comfortably crossed, on the bed of the guest room. He looked up when Maggie tapped on the door, then put aside the newspaper he'd been reading. He must have found an outdated issue left on the dresser and sat down to glance through it. His hair was wet but clean, and he'd been buffing it one-handed with another towel. A few droplets of water still glistened in the sprinkling of curly hair on his chest. He hadn't shaved, though an abundance of razors and other supplies was available in the bathroom, but Maggie supposed she shouldn't expect a tiger to change his stripes. He looked virile, barely civilized and surprisingly attractive sitting there on the bed in a warm circle of lamplight while the oncoming storm rattled the windows. On the pastel pink coverlet, he looked incongruously male.

His black eyes flickered over her, too, taking in the soft jumpsuit that covered Maggie from chin to ankles. He smothered a smile. "I was reading your column," he said, indicating the newspaper. Easily, he sat up and swung his legs over the side of the bed. "Your opinion on thank-you notes for wedding gifts is pretty hard-line."

Determined to remain serene, Maggie entered the room and put the tray on the night table. "You'd be surprised how many newly married couples forget to communicate their thank-yous. It's an important issue."

"Oh, I agree," he said mildly. He took the moment to appraise her attire again. Belatedly, Maggie realized it displayed all of her slender curves to perfection. Mick appeared to enjoy the view.

Maggie steeled herself as she poured his beer into a tall glass and handed it to Mick. "I want to thank you," she said at last. "Formally, I mean, for helping to find Elizabeth."

"Don't forget you helped me out of a tight situation, too."

Maggie shook her head. "That was nothing. What you did was—it was very brave."

"No, ma'am," he said, accepting the beer. "Pulling the kid out of the rocks was the easy part. Facing a frantic mother was no picnic. You slugged me, remember?" He rubbed his cheek in memory.

"I apologize," Maggie said at once, embarrassed and contrite. "It was inexcusable."

"I'd like to hear an excuse anyway."

She pretended not to understand and picked up her own drink. "I appreciate what you did for my daughter—especially in the face of my rudeness to you on the beach. I couldn't have rescued her myself. I just—well, thank you."

He sipped his beer and relaxed back into the pillows on the bed, recrossing his legs and getting comfortable. "You're welcome," he said simply. "Now maybe you'd like to tell me what's going on."

Maggie blinked. "Going on?"

"Yeah," he said. "First I get accused of kidnapping. Then I'm told I have an accomplice and you go splashing into the ocean like I've sprouted horns and a tail. Oh, and I forgot about the part where the phone rings and you don't answer it. Unless I miss my guess, Maggie Kincaid, there's something fishy going on around here."

Maggie took a sip of her Scotch and swallowed it. "I don't know what gives you that idea."

"Lady," he said with great patience. "I watched you lose control this afternoon. You don't look like the type who does that very often. Something's wrong."

"I thought Elizabeth had wandered off, that's all. I was frightened."

"Frightened doesn't describe the look on your face this afternoon," he shot back. "Or the way you're spilling that drink on the rug right now."

Maggie hastily righted her glass. When Mick passed her the towel he'd been using on his head, she bent down and daubed up the splashes of Scotch, glad he couldn't see her expression.

When the rug couldn't get any cleaner, Mick reached for her arm. Gently authoritative, he forced Maggie to stand up. Like a conscientious parent, he disengaged the glass of Scotch from her hand. "This stuff will only make things worse," he said, setting the glass back onto the tray with his own. He guided her to the bed. "Sit down," he ordered. "And tell me about it."

Maggie realized how much she wanted to sit down. Her knees gave way, in fact, and she just managed to sit on the corner of the bed without calling attention to her unsteadiness.

"Well?" he prodded, sitting back to listen.

Maggie knotted her hands and shook her head. "It's just—I am concerned about something, but it's really not—"

"It's none of my business. Right. Well, saving you from drowning and digging your kid out from a collapsing cave isn't my business either, but—"

"I understand your frustration," Maggie held up her hand to quiet him. "Believe me," she said, "it would be better if you didn't get involved."

Mick's black eyes were sharp, steady and intelligent. "Why?"

"You—you could get hurt."

Apparently that was funny. Mick laughed. Really laughed. He put his head back and hooted. "Miss Margaret," he said in a little while, shaking his head at her, "do I look like the kind of guy who gets nervous when he hears a line like that?''

"No," she admitted uneasily, "but—"

"Look," he said, leaning forward and taking her hand in his, "somebody like you can't say anything that's going to surprise somebody like me. You know what I mean?"

Maggie looked at him. Though attired in a luxurious towel and seated on a very expensive, custom-made coverlet, Mick Spiderelli was still a thug. He looked every inch a criminal. A tough, no-nonsense, capable killer who could also cuddle a little child when the situation warranted. And the light but warm grip of his hands felt strangely reassuring.

"What's the story?" he asked.

Maggie frowned. She had nothing to lose, really.

"Start from the beginning," he coached, releasing her.

Thunder rumbled again, sending a shudder through the house. In that moment, Maggie experienced the sensation of being oddly separated from the rest of the world. The storm had somehow isolated them from the troubles of mankind. Here they were alone. Surely she had little to fear from a man who had just given her back her daughter. For that she would be forever grateful. Maggie owed him an explanation, at least. And Mick Spiderelli—big and capable and very strong—seemed like a good ally just then.

"What is it?" he pressed, still gently. "Husband?"

Maggie shook her head. "I'm not married."

"Ex-husband?"

"No," she said. "I've never been married."

He glanced at the doorway toward the voices of his own son and Elizabeth. As if in question, he made a motion to shut the door.

Maggie nodded, and when it was quietly closed she looked down at her knotted hands and said, "I wasn't married to Elizabeth's father. Until lately, I considered that relationship long-dead.''

Mick sat back and got comfortable. "Sounds like this is gonna be quite a story.''

Suddenly Maggie wanted to tell it, too. She'd kept everything bottled up tightly, afraid she'd release an evil genie if she allowed even part of the tale to escape. Slowly, she said, "It will seem out of character, I suppose. I must look like some kind of puritan throwback to you, but—well, I haven't always been. I have a stimulating career and a wonderful, supportive family, but a few years ago I—I had a love affair. I didn't know it at the time, but the man was—well, I guess you might call him a fortune hunter. Ben Bratton was his name. We became engaged and I thought he loved me, but something happened to prove he didn't care for me as much as he cared for my family's money. We broke up. I didn't handle it very well. I guess I'm more fragile than I—well, suffice it to say I was distressed and upset by what happened.''

"And?''

"And...in the weeks after he left, I discovered I was pregnant.''

"By choice?''

"No,'' she said, hesitantly. "I always wanted a child, but I hadn't planned on starting a family until after I was married. But even though I was alone, I was glad. I suppose I needed someone who was mine—who would always be a part of my life.''

He watched her face directly and didn't speak.

Maggie looked away. "So I forgot about my love affair and Elizabeth came into my life. And she is such a joy!'' Maggie smiled. Fervently, she said, "I was meant for this! I love being a mother. I was never good with men. But motherhood is something I'm good at.''

"Did you tell the guy? That he was the father?''

"N-no," she said, sobering once again.

"Afraid?"

Maggie nodded. "Of what Ben might do, yes. He— You see, he was paid to leave me."

Mick tilted his head. His expression remained reserved, but his eyes narrowed suddenly.

Maggie sighed uncomfortably. "You'd have to know my uncle to understand all this. My uncle is the head of the Kincaid family—he's Joseph B. Kincaid, the boss of all of us, a powerful man who wants the best for himself and everyone connected with the family. My parents travel a lot—they're physicians for a world hunger organization, and I grew up in my uncle's house. He saw that I was educated and helped me get my job. He always showed an interest in what I did."

"You mean he meddles."

Maggie smiled a little. "All right, yes. Sometimes he has interfered where he has no business, but in Ben's case—"

"Let me guess," said Mick. "Uncle Joe saw your boyfriend's real motive and paid him to take a hike."

Maggie winced. "Your wording is crude, but—"

"But accurate."

Unwillingly, she nodded. "Yes, exactly accurate. J.B. has a nose for frauds and he paid Ben a hundred thousand dollars in cash to get out of my life." With a bitterness that surprised herself, Maggie said, "It was insulting how little money it took to get him to leave. But Ben likes living well and socializing in the right circles. And now—"

"He's run through the hundred thou' like water," Mick guessed. "And he's back for more."

Startled, Maggie asked, "Do *you* know Ben?"

Mick laughed. "No, but I know the type. Did he go direct to your uncle or through the back door to you this time?"

"To me," Maggie said. "Somehow he found out I had a child. He might have hired someone and then done some mathematics. He knows Elizabeth is his daughter, and he wants to share custody."

"I take it he's not interested in experiencing the joys of hands-on fatherhood?"

"No, I'm sure he really doesn't really want a child. Elizabeth has a trust fund that Ben is very interested in managing."

"I see. Can he be sure she's his kid? I mean, the miracles of modern medicine can't prove beyond a shadow of a doubt that—"

"Ben knows." Maggie fought to keep her voice level. "He knows me. I'm not the kind of woman who—I just *wouldn't.*"

"You hadn't slept with anyone else?"

"Of course not. I'm not—I don't do that sort of thing!" Flustered, she began, "Why, I was—when I first met Ben I had never—"

"You were a virgin?"

She winced at the word. "Yes," she said, and blushed.

"Good lord," said Mick, laughing. "What convent did you attend, Miss Margaret?"

"No convent. I'm just not—well, I'm just not a sexual person."

Mick eyed her askance, his cynical smile fading. Bluntly, he said, "Why'd you pick him to hit the sheets with? What was so appealing about the guy?"

Maggie felt her face burning pink, and she turned away from him. "Nothing, I suppose. Ben is attractive, of course. Very charming despite being a bit of a social climber. But he—he made me feel special. Underneath everything he's insecure, and I guess I'm that way myself. I suppose I was extremely gullible. I knew he wasn't going to make a fairy-tale husband—I'd given up on the Prince Charming dream long ago! He wanted social position which my family could give him, and I—well, I wanted children more than anything. I wasn't looking for eternal devotion. I thought he'd give me children and leave me alone to enjoy them." Maggie glanced at Mick, wondering if he could possibly understand. "I thought we were compatible, and I thought that was enough."

"You could have shopped for a father in a singles' bar," Mick said, "and avoided a hell of a lot of trouble."

"That's exactly what I would have done," Maggie replied. "If I'd been braver."

For an odd moment, Mick didn't respond to that, and studying him for a reaction, Maggie thought that Ben's qualifications for fatherhood certainly paled by comparison to the man lolling so casually on the bed beside her. The difference in genes alone was staggering. Ben's good looks, his sharp, dry wit, his interest in the arts—ballet and classical music—rendered him a good candidate for passing cultured qualities on to a child. Elizabeth had many interests and already showed a gift for the piano.

But Maggie found herself wondering how things might have turned out if her child had been a boy. Would Ben's genes have created an equally wonderful son? If Maggie had cold-bloodedly looked for a man to father a boy, Ben would have come in a distant second to a rugged man-of-action like Mick Spiderelli. Whether battling water on a choppy ocean, climbing through jungle underbrush or just drinking a beer in the kitchen, Mick acted as if he *belonged*.

And perhaps he did. Maggie guessed he'd feel at home nearly anywhere he chose to go. There were men like that in the world, she knew, men who had earned their right to swagger by virtue of the things they'd seen and done. Mick was clearly one of them. Any boy would put his life on the line for a father like that.

Mick said, "You're in a fix, all right, Miss Margaret."

Snapping out of her embarrassing reverie, Maggie said, "Yes."

"Does Uncle Joe know what's going on now?"

"That brings up another angle of my situation. I haven't spoken to my uncle," said Maggie flatly, "in five and a half years."

"Oho," said Mick. "Have you gotten yourself a good lawyer? There's got to be a legal way out of this."

"It's not quite that simple," Maggie said, uneasily.

"There's more?"

She nodded and cleared her throat, hesitating. "I haven't told anyone this last part. You'll have to—it's very upsetting, and you must swear you won't—I mean, it's . . ."

"Yes?"

Maggie put one shaking hand to her forehead. "It's very embarrassing, really. I mean—"

Gently, Mick interrupted. He said one word. "Blackmail?"

Maggie gasped and stared at him. "How did you come to *that* conclusion?"

Mick's mouth formed a grim sort of smile. "Let's just say the concept isn't unknown to me. He threatened you with something, right?"

Maggie got up off the bed. For the first time in several minutes she was aware of being alone in a bedroom with a man she didn't know. "Look," she began, "perhaps I'd better not get into this. You've been very kind to listen, but—"

"Kind, nothing," he retorted, catching her wrist and finding her flesh icy cold. "I'm damn curious. Sit down and talk."

"Please, I—"

Mick held fast. "He'd have to have something hot to put Dear Miss Margaret out of business. Dear Abby survived her own divorce, if I remember correctly, and lord knows how many politicians have emerged unscathed from all manner of scandal. He'd have to get hold of something really wild.''

Maggie twisted, imprisoned in his grip. Her throat felt horribly tight. "Please—"

Mick saw her tears start and released her. "Is that it?" he asked in the resulting silence. "Blackmail?"

Maggie hugged herself miserably and nodded. "Yes."

Just remembering the awful night Ben Bratton had come to her, she began to tremble. He had looked so different from before. Greed had gleamed in his face and made him look brutish. He'd forced his way into her home by threatening to break down the door. With Elizabeth sleeping peacefully upstairs, Maggie had let him in. Though horrified by what he proposed, Maggie listened to every word, praying only that he'd leave without disturbing her daughter.

"What's he got?" Mick asked.

"Pictures," Maggie whispered. "Photographs."

"Of you?"

"Yes," she said, eyes closed.

Mick swore under his breath, then asked, "Bedroom stuff?"

Maggie sat down on the bed again, her legs too shaky to support her any longer. In a humiliated rush, she said, "I had no idea they existed. Really, I would never submit myself to that kind of— How he did it is beyond me!"

"Drugs?"

"What?"

"Were you doing drugs at the time?"

"Doing—?" Maggie lifted her head and stared. *"Me?"*

"Forget I mentioned it," Mick said, amused. Then, frowning, he tried to envision the scenario. "Hidden camera, then?"

"It must have been. I don't know for sure. I—I only slept with Ben twice. We were engaged by then, of course—"

"Of course," Mick said with a trace of mocking humor. "He must have taken pictures the second time you were together?"

"Yes, but he didn't show me the photographs until just a few weeks ago."

"When he suggested trading pictures for a crack at the trust fund. What did you tell him?"

"Nothing. I didn't say anything. I needed time to think. I was—I felt stripped." Shaking, she whispered, "Humiliated and—and, oh, so damn stupid!"

Mick shrugged. "It happens."

"Not to me!" Maggie cried. "I felt horrible. Weak and stupid and helpless."

"You wouldn't be the first."

Her voice cracked. "I *hate* it!"

Instantly, she controlled herself, choking back the emotion. Maggie caught sight of herself in the vanity mirror then. Her face was pale and even she could see the fear and pain in her gray eyes. She looked away abruptly. In a voice that was exasperatingly small, she said, "And I felt guilty, too."

"Guilty?" Finally Mick looked surprised. "Why guilty?"

"Because I'd taken advantage of him," she said, unsteadily. "I used him, in a way. I got what I wanted—the child I'd been hoping for for so long. Ben just turned the tables on me, that's all."

Mick laughed shortly. "Forget it, Miss Margaret. Your buddy Ben was looking for a quick buck long before he was offered the payoff from Uncle Joe. You shouldn't feel guilty."

Maggie shook her head. "I can't help it. Sometimes I think I deserve to be punished."

Mick snorted. "You been reading *Faust* lately?"

"It's a little like that," Maggie admitted. "Elizabeth is so wonderful that I never thought twice about how she'd been conceived. I made a kind of pact with the devil, and now it's coming back to haunt me."

"You're afraid of the publicity?"

"Not so much for myself. J.B. would hate it. And Elizabeth, of course."

Mick nodded. "It could get pretty rough on her, I guess."

Quaking inside, Maggie whispered, "I was such a fool." She realized that she hadn't been as much in command of herself as she thought, for she was feeling queerly dizzy and found herself swaying.

Mick reacted swiftly. He reached for her glass of Scotch and helped her take a sip. Her hands trembled, and her teeth chattered on the rim. She was glad he held on to it for her. She took a sip, swallowed wrong and choked.

And then—like an idiot—she burst into tears.

Crying women didn't fluster him, Mick thought as he put the glass out of reach. In his business, he encountered them with fairly frequent regularity. He had expected Maggie Kincaid to break down long before this. She put her face in her hands and cried with all the stops pulled out, but he remained calm. He had learned a long time ago that the safest thing he could do was shut up and nine times out of ten most weepers cleaned up their acts by themselves.

But then Mick had put the glass aside and—not even realizing he was breaking one of his hardest and fastest professional rules—he'd touched her. She looked so small and forlorn and beautiful. With his fingertips, he smoothed back the fine wisps of Maggie's dark hair from her temples. She didn't flinch, overwhelmed by her own emotion just then, and he traced a thoughtful whorl on her cheek with his thumb. She cried like an overtired toddler, weakly and blindly. Mick caressed a spot just beneath her delicate jaw, and he found her pulse there. It fluttered like the wings of a captured butterfly.

Oddly, Mick found himself thinking of another beautiful woman, one who had never seemed so far away.

After three more dry, racking sobs, Maggie pulled herself together. For a moment she quivered with the effort of self-control, and then drew herself up sharply, away from his touch.

She hiccoughed once and said ferociously, "I hate crying!"

Mick smiled a little. "Self-sufficient all the way, aren't you?"

She wiped her eyes hurriedly, and avoided looking at him. "I don't know about that. I'm not feeling so damn self-sufficient at the moment."

Mick knew there were a lot of glib, macho answers to that kind of observation. And as she sat on the bed just an arm's length away, brushing little jewel-like tears off the porcelain perfection of her face, he almost offered a few of them. But this particular female, cautioned a voice in the back of Mick's mind, was the worst kind of woman to get mixed up with. She was sweet, for God's sake. She was the sort of lady a man automatically held doors and carried packages for. Well-bred and feminine, and not the least bit streetwise.

She was the kind of woman who got into a man's system and stayed there.

Females like Maggie Kincaid weren't supposed to exist anymore. At least that had been Mick's conclusion. Women were tough and resilient these days. They didn't need protection or devotion or even the intimacy with a capital "I" that everyone was talking about for a while. Mick had found that women were easy to do business with nowadays. Get the job done, that was it. After a meeting, one particular Amazon had slipped her company business card down the front of his jeans. Even sex could be businesslike.

And sex was exactly what Mick found himself thinking about as he sat on the bed and listened to Maggie Kincaid's irregular breathing, as he smelled the sun and seawater in her hair, as he watched her slender fingers nervously entwine. He saw a hundred fascinating little details in her—the pale curve of her cheek, the soft gray light in her brimming eyes, the lush plum color of her lips, the milky skin of her throat and the way it melted into the full roundness of her breasts.

She'd have been desirable under any circumstances. A lovely, gentle woman with a tender heart. But she'd gotten mixed up with the wrong element and now she was a lamb—a lamb who had wandered away from the fold, too close to a hungry wolf. And the only thing that could save her from the jaws of one such predator was a bigger wolf.

Like himself.

She needed help, all right. At least that's what she wanted him to think.

Could her innocent lamb routine be a ruse, Mick wondered? Surely nobody was as naive as she pretended to be.

Mick considered the possibilities, soberly. How likely were the chances that a rich and powerful family like the Kincaids could harbor as pretty and proper a lady as Maggie appeared to be? Perhaps the whole Miss Margaret persona was a fake.

Mick reached out his forefinger and touched the trembling point of her chin. He tipped her face higher, and she obeyed, half-puzzled, half-mesmerized as he studied her features. Slowly, he smoothed his fingers along the underside of her jaw until he found the downy softness of her hairline, just behind her ear. He felt something hot flicker inside himself, something both angry and erotic.

"What are you thinking?" she whispered, her eyes wide as she searched his expression.

"It doesn't pay to think all the time," he said. "Sometimes I have to listen to my gut."

There was one way of finding out how much of her story was true. Mick ran his fingers into her silky hair and pulled her head close. He brushed her lips with his to measure his own interest in the plan.

"Wait," she said.

"Nope. Come here." He swooped, and took her mouth. Maggie sketched a quick movement of dissent, pressing both her hands against his chest, but Mick ignored it and delved deeper into her mouth. She tasted sweet, but she fought him, struggling to push out of his arms, to turn her head away. For an instant he wanted to roll and press her down onto the coverlet, to unwrap her demure jumpsuit and seek the warmest places of her body with his hands, his mouth, to find out how much of her was real.

But she wasn't going to allow that. He could feel it as she wrenched in his arms. And suddenly Mick wanted very much to have her any way he could.

Instinctively, he gentled his kiss. Coaxingly, Mick slanted his mouth across Maggie's meltingly delicious lips. With his fingers in her hair, he tilted her head this way and that to make the contact of their mouths more perfect, more tantalizing. His tongue found hers and teased until he felt Maggie start to yield. Slowly, Mick lay back in the pillows, drawing Maggie with him until her soft, slender body settled naturally against his own.

She could have escaped just then. She could have scratched him or kicked and terminated the whole thing then and there. She'd walloped him once before. But Mick felt her willpower crumble. Her limbs lost their tension. Her lips turned liquid against his. He felt her heartbeat skitter and race out of control. She wasn't cool anymore. Suddenly she was melting against his mouth, turning warm in his arms.

Foolishly, the little liar began to kiss him back.

Four

———

The contour of Mick's powerful body beneath hers, the searing heat of his mouth and the sensual rush of her own heart, all combined to overwhelm Maggie at first. She felt the warmth of him steal into her bones and the languor or her own subtle shift in emotions invade her mind, clouding her powers of reason. He loosened her hair. He touched her face. Mick murmured to her, and something twisted in the pit of Maggie's stomach like a living creature. The sensation nearly turned her inside out, ridding Maggie of her common sense. Was it desire? What was this magical experience?

It felt wonderful to be held, to be coaxed, to be in charge and yet dizzyingly out of control. It was intoxicating.

It was scary, too. Frightened by her instinctive reaction to the man, Maggie pressed both hands flat against Mick's shoulders and pushed, insisting on escape. He resisted, tightening his embrace for a heart-stopping second, arching his body until her own rode snugly against him, drawing her mouth deeper into his kiss. Maggie couldn't breathe, couldn't think, and for a ghastly moment she didn't want to. But finally he obeyed her wish. Mick loosened his hold, allowing their lips to part centimeter by slow centimeter until they were face to face and motionless.

"Wait," Maggie said, maddeningly breathless and unable to tear her eyes away from his. "Please. I'm not—I can't do this kind of thing."

"Come on," he murmured, catching her silky hair between his fingers. "You can't be as timid as you pretend to be."

"Not timid," she said, unsteadily. "Just unwilling. I'm not—I'm not comfortable with this." So tightly were they lying together that she noticed she could feel the quick beat of his heart against her breast. The realization struck her as so intimate that for a moment Maggie couldn't put her next words together. "Please understand," she said at last. "It's not you. It's—I'm not—the children might come in and—"

"The kids are busy," he said, his voice a murmur in her ear as he nuzzled her throat. Slowly, he found the delicate lobe of her ear and nibbled. "We may never get a chance like this again."

Maggie shuddered a sigh. The sensations he evoked were heavenly. "Please," she said again, afraid of the way she was reacting. "Please, don't."

With his free hand, Mick tipped Maggie's face up to his. She was startled to find his expression oddly hard. In his eyes blazed a curious—almost suspicious—light. Even his voice lost its warmth. He said, "Are you for real?"

Maggie pried her way out of his arms and got to her feet. "Of course I'm for real." She laughed uncertainly. She probably sounded drunk, but she couldn't help herself. "You must think I'm horribly out of step with the times.

I'm not a modern woman, am I? Look, would you mind just forgetting about the last five minutes? I don't know what's gotten into me."

Voice low, Mick said, "Some people call it passion."

"I call it flustered!" She pulled her hair back tight and searched in it for the loosened pins. Nervously, she chattered. "Goodness, what a day it's been! I must have lost my wits. Really, I'm not this kind of person at all."

Mick remained on the bed. He folded his hands behind his head and studied her. "You said that before. Surely you don't mean it."

"Yes, of course. I wasn't cut out for—for the boudoir." She tried to laugh again. "I'm a mother, not a lover."

"You could be both."

"Some women can. Not me."

Mick went on watching her, which just made Maggie all the more nervous. Quietly, he said, "Who did this to you, Maggie?"

"What?"

"Was it Ben who tightened the straitjacket? Or Uncle Joe who made you worship the rules of etiquette above all else? At first I thought it was an act. But you can't even lose your temper, can you? You've got a grip on your composure that's unbreakable."

"There's nothing wrong with me," Maggie said firmly. "The focus of my life isn't sex, that's all."

"So you've sworn off anything that's remotely sensual."

Maggie straightened her spine with a snap. She glared at him. "I'm not a floozie, Mr. Spiderelli."

He laughed outright at the word, but gave up the argument for the time being. He rolled off the bed in a single, lithe motion that bespoke a body in superb physical condition. The towel clasped around his lean hips nearly failed its job, but he caught it casually. As he got to his feet, Maggie realized again how tall Mick stood over her. His legs were impossibly long and obviously well muscled, and his shoulders made no secret of their strength, either. His black hair was nearly dry, but it was wildly curly—as untamed as he seemed to be just then. For a few minutes Maggie had allowed herself to forget what he was—a strong man in a violent line of work. What kinds of crimes had he committed with those powerful hands of his? The same hands that had come so close to caressing her? Unconsciously, Maggie took a pace backward.

He tweaked a lock of her hair loose and curled it between his fingers. He smiled coldly at the same time. "Don't look so scared all of a sudden. I'll leave you alone now. I had to find out something, that's all."

"Find out—? What are you talking about?"

Mick circled the bed in a saunter, heading for the bathroom with the air of a victorious quarterback after the big game. "Look, don't take this the wrong way, Miss Margaret, but you didn't exactly add up. You talk like a character out of Jane Austen but sure look like a woman of the eighties. I had to make sure you were telling the truth. Forgive my methods."

"Your *methods*!" Maggie sputtered. "You—you mean you were playacting just now?"

"To see how you'd react. Sure."

"Why, you—you big thug!"

He grinned, bracing his bare shoulder against the doorframe to watch her rage build. "Now, now, it's not polite to call people names." He wagged one finger at her. "You've got a hell of a suspicious setup here, you know. A seductively beautiful woman hiding in some kind of Caribbean palace starts telling me about a meddling uncle, a dastardly fiancé, her own virginity and some dirty pictures taken when she least expected—"

"*You* mentioned virginity, not me!"

"Does it matter who said it first? In my business, I've learned it pays to separate truth from fiction as soon as possible."

"Did kissing me solve your dilemma?" she cracked.

"It helped. At least part of your story is true. You're every bit as unsullied as you claim."

"Oh?" Harshly, Maggie demanded, "You're absolutely sure about that?"

"Yep. I gave it my best shot. I'm told I'm irresistible when I want to be, but you resisted with all the willpower of a virtuous princess in a tower."

Maggie snapped her mouth shut. She was quivering like an arrow just shot from a crossbow, but perhaps he didn't see that. Mick didn't know how close he'd come to dissolving her willpower completely. Thank heavens she'd managed to break out of his arms in time. But now it seemed he'd been faking, too, and Maggie found that galling.

"Mr. Best Shot, if it weren't storming outside," she said in a low voice, "I'd throw you out on your irresistible ear."

He folded his arms over his bare chest. His dark eyes gleamed. "Is the storm your only reason for holding back? Or did I stir up something after all?"

Maggie gathered all her outrage into one withering glance. "Nothing whatsoever!"

She wrenched open the bedroom door and marched out, head high. Her glorious exit was spoiled, however, by a distinct laugh from the thug in the bathroom.

She proceeded directly to the kitchen, yanking the remaining pins from her hair. While the wind howled and the rain pounded on the skylight above her head, Maggie ranted to herself in a furious whisper.

"A *hit man*!" she muttered, hurling a loaf of bread onto the cutting board. "I'm a civilized, gracious, *intelligent* woman, and I spilled my most intimate secrets to a—an oafish, oversexed executioner! He's a jerk! A bully! I'll bet he carried a personalized garrote in his pocket!—when he's wearing enough clothes to *have* a pocket, of course! My stars, what will happen next?''

She had only to ask the question when something did happen. The lights went out.

A jagged flash of lightning exploded just yards from where Maggie stood, followed by a tremendous crash of thunder that rocked the room and tore an instinctive shriek from Maggie's throat. The knife clattered from her hand. Then the electricity flickered once and died.

''Terrific,'' Maggie said, to the resulting darkness.

Over the drumming of rain, she heard Mick's voice calling from the bedrooms. ''Maggie?'' he shouted. ''You okay?''

''I'm in the kitchen!'' she bellowed back. ''I think the generator was struck by lightning.''

He said something unintelligible in reply, but when Maggie heard both children giggling she assumed all was well. The kitchen was pitch black, so Maggie felt her way along the counter and rummaged in the emergency drawer for candles and matches. She had lighted a short, fragrant candle by the time Mick arrived with the children. Spider was riding piggyback, and Elizabeth was smiling shyly in Mick's arms. In her small hands, she held a fine crystal cigarette lighter, which they had apparently used to find their way through the house. The flickering light illuminated Elizabeth's pale but happy face. She looked excited and pleased to find herself in the middle of an adventure.

''This is neat,'' Spider proclaimed, clambering from his father's shoulders onto the nearest stool. ''No lights, no electricity—it's like the Swiss Family Robinson!''

''The Robinsons would have killed for some of the amenities around here,'' Mick noted, reaching for the wine rack. He pulled down a bottle of champagne and studied the label. Apparently prepared to ignore the hot words he'd just exchanged with her in the bedroom, he said, "It's a modest little wine, but it'll have to do, I suppose. Shall I pop your cork, Miss Margaret?"

He had laughter in his eyes which Maggie tried to quell with a cold stare. She removed the bottle from his grasp. "Champagne doesn't go with peanut butter sandwiches. You'll have to rough it, I'm afraid."

"Peanut butter?" Mick pulled a pathetic face. "We're stranded in paradise! Surely a woman with your refined good taste could rustle up something more exciting than peanut butter!"

"No electricity," Maggie pointed out. "No cooking."

"The stove's gas," said Mick, damnably sharp-eyed. "Come on, Miss Margaret, let's have a feast."

"That's quite impossible."

"Why?" Mick caught sight of her face. "Hold the phone! Tell me the truth, Miss Margaret. Do you know a saucepan from a corkscrew?"

Maggie flushed. "I'm not exceptionally talented in the kitchen if you must know, but I—"

"I get the picture," Mick said, laughing rudely. "We're on our own, right? Well, kids? Are you game for some fun on the range? We'll have to cook for ourselves, tonight. Miss Margaret gave the chef a night off."

"See here," Maggie began hotly, "I'm not a complete incompetent. I can certainly poach an egg or—"

"Poached eggs! Lady, we're *hungry*! You probably expect us to choke down tea and watercress, too! We want some real food, right kids? Besides, what else are we going to do on a night like this? Miss Margaret, prepare yourself for the culinary experience of a lifetime!"

"What's culinary?" Elizabeth asked, enchanted by the melodrama unfolding before her.

"Don't mind him," Spider said, dolefully. "When he starts with the big words, you really don't have to listen. He's just talking to himself."

"Button it, brat," Mick said. "And go check the refrigerator. Let's see what we've got to work with! And you, Miss Margaret, had better get out of our way. May I offer you a seat?"

He flung a towel over his forearm, bowed elaborately and held out one of the kitchen stools for her. Maggie saw the look of challenge in his snapping dark eyes and figured she had no choice but to do exactly as he commanded. She sat.

After that, Mick plunged into the plan with gusto. Elizabeth and Spider were with him all the way. They raided the refrigerator and spread all the available food on the counter. Mick got himself a beer and Elizabeth poured lemonade for herself and Spider, and the three of them happily set about preparing an evening meal.

Maggie lit more candles and watched from the sidelines. Mick, she noticed, was newly combed and dressed in his own shorts and a shirt he must have found in the guest room. It was a plain gray, well-worn Boston College sweatshirt, no doubt left behind by a long-departed Kincaid guest. Somehow, though, the simple shirt looked magnificent on Mick. He had pushed the sleeves up over his tanned forearms, and his hair curled tantalizingly against the stretched-out collar. He was truly an awe-inspiring specimen of a man.

He supervised the children with an offhand manner, allowing them to make a mess of the kitchen and not providing too much direction. He lounged on the stool or strolled between the two youngsters making remarks and laughing with them while they measured water and pasta, washed vegetables and built a fruit salad. Then Mick showed his culinary prowess by whipping together a fantastic white sauce. With the panache of an expert he next sautéed scallops and shrimp. Spider crunched on carrots matter-of-factly, Elizabeth looked enthralled by the unusual goings-on. The three of them sang silly songs and told knock-knock jokes and gradually made Maggie feel like Ebenezer Scrooge on Christmas Eve.

She figured out his scheme after just a few minutes, of course. The hurricane sounded worse and worse by the minute, but Mick intended to keep the children's minds off the storm. And he succeeded! They laughed when the thunder crashed overhead. They opened the window and caught hailstones in a saucepan, then added them to the pasta water. When another stupendous bolt of lightning exploded so close the whole house shook with the impact, Mick was merrily throwing spaghetti against the wall to see if it was cooked properly yet.

"I learned all my technique in Brooklyn, Miss Margaret, in case you're thinking of hiring me to replace the family chef."

And when the food was ready, no one sat down at the table with napkins and silver.

"Come on, Miss Margaret! Haven't you ever been on a picnic?"

"Not indoors," Maggie retorted. "And certainly not with messy food like pasta."

"Then you haven't lived," Mick pronounced. "You've got a treat in store. Here. Take some extra napkins if you're worried about dribbling."

Both children carried bowls and forks into the living room and really did make a picnic on the floor. Elizabeth sat cross-legged and tried her best to be civilized, but Spider sprawled on his belly and soon had Elizabeth sucking the long noodles into her mouth one strand at a time. They chortled like wicked gremlins over their appalling table manners, but Maggie held her tongue. She saw that Elizabeth was practically drunk with pleasure. That sight was better than anything Maggie had seen in a long time.

Mick brought the rest of the meal and a couple of bottles of beer into the living room. "How about it, Miss Margaret?" he asked, casting a mocking look down at her. "A beer with your dinner? Or will a brew like this wound your tender sensibilities?"

Maggie found herself struggling not to smile at him from her position on the floor. "I don't care for beer very much," she said. "Let's open champagne. There's probably a cold bottle in the refrigerator."

He laughed, jogged back to the kitchen and soon returned. He popped open the foaming bottle, sending the children scrambling to find the cork. Then Mick plunked down on the sofa cushions they had spread on the floor and proceeded to pour champagne with flair into the two slender glasses he held in one hand. When he had passed one of the drinks to her, Maggie lifted her glass and caught his eye in the candlelight.

In that instant, Maggie saw a glimmer, a glimpse, the smallest of hints that Mick wasn't everything he appeared to be. There was something underneath his wisecracking facade. Maybe it was the way he treated his son, maybe it was his innate gentleness with Elizabeth, or perhaps it was the briefest flash of surprise she saw reflected in his eyes when he looked at her—as though he expected another woman to be sitting so cozily near him in the half-darkness.

Maggie warmed to him just then. He wasn't as shallow as he pretended. There was something more, perhaps even something troubled that lurked beneath Mick Spiderelli's tough exterior. Wonderingly, and still shyly too, Maggie smiled at him. The quick breezelike surprise left Mick's face as swiftly as it had come, and he grinned back at her, his rogue's attitude back in place. While the children giggled over their food, Mick and Maggie shared that single, acknowledging look, raised their glasses in simultaneous toast to well-kept secrets, and then they drank champagne together.

"Dig in," said Mick, diving for his plate like a starving beast.

With somewhat more restraint, Maggie reached for her portion, too. She sampled the dish daintily and smiled. It tasted marvelous. Delighted, Maggie ate with an appetite.

When they had all eaten their fill, Maggie looked around the circle of faces in the candlelight and decided they didn't look so much like the participants in a Roman orgy as they did a somewhat oddly matched, but definitely contented family. The thought wouldn't go away, either. After a while she realized the storm had passed, though she hadn't been aware of when it happened. The thunder grew distant, and the only sound that penetrated the villa was the rattle of half-hearted rain on the roof.

At last Mick ordered the children to return the dishes to the kitchen and go brush their teeth. "Bedtime," he said. "Almost midnight."

"Must we go to bed?" Elizabeth begged, catching his arm familiarly.

"Yes. No arguing either, Sis. You're worn out."

Elizabeth's face clouded with disappointment. "But—will you be here in the morning?"

Mick grinned and tousled her head. "Unless your mom throws me out, yes."

Elizabeth came to Maggie and hugged her around the neck. Maggie hugged back and heard Elizabeth's whisper. "Don't throw him out, Mama. He's fun."

Maggie squeezed her daughter. "I won't. Now run along. Make Spider feel at home."

"I already know where everything is," said Spider at once. "I don't need her help."

Mick caught the boy in his arms. "Be nice," he said. "Give me a kiss." And when the boy had obliged, Mick grinned and said. "Now beat it."

The two children scampered away.

Maggie gazed after them fondly. She did not move except to pick up her glass once more. She felt warm and well fed and ever so slightly intoxicated by the wine.

Mick leaned forward and poured the last drops of champagne into her glass. "Well, Miss Margaret?" he asked softly. "Did we horrify you with our bad manners and finger food?"

"The food was delicious," Maggie replied, sipping from her glass. "And some occasions call for a relaxing of table etiquette."

Mick smiled, watching her drain the last drops of wine. "I *thought* I caught you relaxing this evening."

"If you're going to make fun of me—"

"Nothing of the kind. It's nice to see you looking so contented, all of a sudden. And I was glad to see you lose your temper earlier, too."

"Could we drop that subject before it gets started?"

"Sure. It's just good to know that you're human."

Maggie threw caution to the wind. "I'd much rather talk about you."

"Me?" The idea caught him off guard. "Boring subject," he said.

"Maybe not. I'm curious. You did rather appear in our lives like a tornado."

"All right." He shrugged. "What d'you want to hear? I went to PS 48 and played stickball in—"

"We can skip the *David Copperfield* lines."

"Ah, you want the current stuff."

Maggie wanted very much to ask about Spider's mother. The question had nagged her practically since the moment of Mick's arrival. But suddenly—sitting alone with him in the quiet salon—Maggie was afraid to pry. She was afraid of what she might hear.

Mick saw the indecision cross her face. His smile turned cold. He asked, "How much do you already know?"

Maggie swallowed. "Nothing, really. I—I shouldn't have opened this discussion. Please accept my apologies. It was very rude. I'll go help the children get ready for bed now if—"

She moved to get up, but Mick reached out quick as a tiger and seized her wrist. The grip hurt! He pulled her down until their faces were barely a foot apart.

"Suppose you tell me how much you've already figured out."

Mick's voice was low, but more commanding than if he'd shouted at her. Kneeling awkwardly before him, Maggie began to tremble, and worse, she knew Mick could feel it, too.

He said, "What has Spider told you?"

Her throat was dry, but she managed to ask, "Spider?"

"Yes. I'm sure he's blabbed some nonsense already. Tell me." Mick jerked her wrist, to emphasize the command. "Tell me now."

Frightened, Maggie stammered, "He—he didn't mean to give away any secrets—"

"Exactly what did the little monster spill?"

"That—that you—"

"Spit it out!"

"That you were a—a hit man."

"A—?" Mick's face changed, and Maggie nearly panicked. She had seen his frustration build, his eyes gleam with anger. But suddenly he laughed. He let Maggie go and roared. "A *hit man*? By God, that kid is pathological! He's outdone himself this time!"

Bewildered, Maggie rubbed her wrist. "What do you mean?"

Mick wagged his head. "Miss Margaret, you're as gullible as they come. At the moment, Spider's the most compulsive liar I've ever run across."

"You mean you're not a—?"

"A hit man? No, I'm sorry to say, I'm not. You actually believed that story?"

"What do you expect?" Maggie demanded, getting her back up. "He's an intelligent young boy, and you're—well, you certainly *look* the part!"

"Do you mean," said Mick, "that you've been afraid of me all this time?"

Maggie calmed herself. Tersely, she said, "I've been terrified."

"Terrified?" He grinned. "You have a funny way of showing it. I seem to remember a moment in the bedroom—"

"There are times," Maggie said, without thinking, "when you seem quite harmless."

"But the rest of the time?" Mick reached across the yard that separated them and took Maggie by her shoulders. He looked deeply into her eyes, a wicked smile playing on his mouth.

Maggie held her breath as he pulled her nearer. Perhaps she was mesmerized by his mocking amusement or the sheer animal handsomeness of him as he bent closer. If Mick kissed her just then, she wasn't sure she would have the strength to resist. She was too relaxed and still reeling from the silly story Spider had made her believe. "The rest of the time," she said unevenly, "I'm scared to death of you."

"Not entirely," guessed Mick, "because of the hit man thing."

He kissed her. Very chastely on the tip of her nose. He didn't touch her body, just leaned close and pulled back when the deed was done. Inside, Maggie felt a warm rivulet of some mysterious element come alive. The reaction happened almost instantly.

She ground her teeth together, trying to quell the disturbance within herself. "Don't tease me, Mr. Spiderelli."

"Say my name," he murmured, voice husky. His lips skimmed along her temple. He breathed a warm current of air along her hairline. "Say it just once."

"Don't," Maggie whispered.

"Say it."

"Please. Mick."

He kissed her again, on the mouth this time. The taste of champagne could not have been so intoxicating as that one tiny brush of his lips against hers. Maggie thought she felt his tongue trace the contour of her upper lip, and she nearly moaned, nearly seized his head in her hands and held him to the kiss a little longer. But Mick drew back.

"Thank you," he said, savoring the taste of her by licking his own lower lip. "I thought I was going to be Hey, You forever. Good night, Maggie."

"Good night?" Maggie blinked, then scrambled to sit up. "Wait!"

He paused in the act of climbing to his feet. Amused, he cocked his head. "Yes?"

"Well, you can't—" she stuttered frantically. "You don't expect me to wonder all night, do you?"

"About what?"

"If you're not a hit man," she asked, "what in the world are you?"

"Ah," said Mick, still on one knee. Thoughtfully, he frowned. "That's a tricky question to answer."

"Try."

He grinned. "I suppose you could say I do little jobs for people."

Maggie was sure Mick was no angel.

He touched Maggie under her chin with his forefinger, causing her to shiver slightly. "No, I don't do errands," he said. "In the business, I'm known as a dirty trickster."

"A—?"

"Not a very charming title, is it? I don't expect you to have heard of my particular line of work. I am usually not employed by members of your social circle, Miss Margaret."

Maggie knitted her brows, trying to recall something Spider had said. "Wiretapping," she remembered, at last. "Bodyguard work."

"Some of that, yes. Mostly electronics, though. Surveillance, but some protection and other jobs." Stroking her throat as if she was an appreciative cat, he said softly, "You have the clearest eyes I've ever seen."

Maggie tried doggedly to keep him on the subject. "What kind of jobs?" she persisted.

He lifted his shoulder in a half-interested shrug, still focused on studying every detail of her face. "Nothing flashy. If a mobster wants his lieutenant framed and put away for a while, I'm the detail man who can arrange a setup."

Maggie's mouth felt very dry all of a sudden. "You arrange setups?"

He smiled slightly. "Yeah, sometimes. Or if a senator's wife suspects the old man is being unfaithful, I keep an eye on him and put a bug in his ear if he starts doing the taxpayers a disservice. I'm an equal opportunity employee, by the way. I work both sides of the fence. The FBI was my client a few times, though they'd rather not publicize the fact. The Dimatto family feels the same way."

Not sure she should believe a word he was saying, Maggie watched his face closely. "You said dirty tricks . . ."

"Yes. My methods aren't always what you'd call kosher."

"You break the law?"

Mick smiled. He caressed her cheek and then slid his fingers into her hair and began, oh, so gently to massage Maggie behind her ear. "My dear lovely Miss Kincaid Publications," he murmured, "are we off the record?"

"I'm not—I'm just curious. You talk like a criminal. Aren't you worried about getting arrested?"

"I like to think I use more finesse than the average crook. And I take the law into my own hands only when I know it deserves to be bent a little. If everyone did it we'd have anarchy, but some situations call for drastic measures. I make decisions on a case-by-case basis."

"You feel entitled to decide which laws can be broken and which laws can't?"

He shrugged. "I didn't go to Harvard Law. I just know I have to live with myself. I make a judgment call when I have to and I live with the consequences. So far, I've done okay."

"Even with the mobster who wanted to frame his lieutenant? You think you were right even then?"

Mick grinned. "Even then. Truth is, Miss Margaret, both the lieutenant *and* the boss went to jail that time."

Maggie swallowed. "I see."

He went on smiling and watching the emotions that must have been revealed on Maggie's face. "Still scared of me, aren't you?"

"N—no," Maggie said.

His caress had stopped. His gaze was fixed upon her with a new intensity, as if a fire kindled inside him was suddenly in want of fuel. A silence stretched. Maggie held rabbit-still, afraid to move for fear she'd break the spell.

They were very much alone in the flickering candlelight. Spider and Elizabeth had ceased making noise, the rain had dwindled to nearly nothing, and Maggie's heartbeat was the only sound she was truly aware of just then. The discovery that Mick wasn't a free-lance executioner came as a relief, of course. But learning his true occupation didn't exactly put her mind at ease. He was not only strong and stubborn but crafty, too. He went on smiling at her, and the look in his eye and the slow curve of his mouth were incredibly sensual.

"What kind of man," she asked quietly, "plays dirty tricks for a living?"

Mick tipped her head higher—gently, but with the confidence of a man who will not be disobeyed. "One who hasn't grown up completely, I suppose," he said mildly.

There it was again, the tone that didn't sound entirely sincere, the verbal jest of a shallow man, one who lived for pleasure and didn't care too much about the consequences. It was an act he slipped into easily. But Maggie felt it *was* an act. The motherly instincts that were so strong within her sensed that Mick was a great deal like his son in one important respect. He liked to think he was a wild, sometimes bad little boy, and inside he kept his innate goodness locked up tight. Something was troubling him, making him keep his facade in place at all times like a suit of armor.

Maggie said, "I suppose you think you're always right, too."

Smiling into her eyes, Mick said, "Yes. I understand human nature."

"Human nature?"

"Sure. People are always my objective. I study their habits and learn their weaknesses. To get what I want, I have to draw up a specific plan of attack and execute it to the letter."

Maggie's voice had a distinctive quaver in it when she spoke again. "Somehow I don't think it could be as easy as you make it sound."

"You're right," Mick said. "Sometimes it gets very complicated."

"And then?"

"Then I rely on instinct."

The air between them almost crackled with tension. And Maggie heard a little voice inside her start to moan with apprehension. As Mick leaned closer, the little voice of common sense rose in pitch until Maggie could hardly hear her own uneven breathing, and the soft words Mick murmured next never made it to her conscious brain. When he caught her loosened hair in his hand and turned her face up to his, Maggie's mind went blank. Desire shone in his eyes, though, she saw that clearly. He couldn't have conveyed his wishes more directly if he'd spoken.

Maggie closed her eyes and let it happen.

He brushed her lips once, drew back, and then came in for the kill. He kissed her thoroughly, savoring the taste and texture of her lips. His tongue rolled hers, explored the cavern of her mouth, teased her and tempted her. Maggie hesitated. Then she began to warm to him, and Mick laughed softly, triumphantly. He curled his fingers more tightly in her hair and delved deeper into her mouth, kissing her with an energy so powerful Maggie shuddered with its force. Dizzily, she clung to him.

Mick traced the line of her jaw with his lips. He pressed petal-soft kisses against the downy hair along her temples. With one hand, he traced the delicate shell of Maggie's ear, then dropped the caress to her shoulder, tracing its roundness with his fingertips. Maggie held her breath, at once dreading and hoping he'd touch her breast. Instead, Mick brushed the soft flesh of her throat and covered each caress with a melting kiss.

Maggie realized she had begun to touch him, too. Beneath her hands, his chest felt like solid muscle, and yet she could feel his heart beating. The strength of it startled her, and Maggie noticed his breathing had turned ragged, too. The tautness of his thighs, pressed against her own, was daunting. And arousing. Had she caused this chained tension in such a seemingly unconquerable man? Mick was on the brink of unleashing something powerful, something vibrant, and that realization was heady indeed.

He caught her off guard. At last too overwrought to control himself, Mick smoothed his hand down her body and cupped one of Maggie's breasts in his warm palm. And before she could protest, he thumbed one of her nipples into a hard, aroused peak through her jumpsuit.

"The lady," he murmured in her ear, "has a few instincts of her own."

He could have pushed her down into the pillows then. Maggie felt a powerful urge to nestle with him on the floor, to let him strip off the cursed fabric that stood between them and a stronger passion than she'd ever known. Incredibly, she longed to feel his whole body against hers. But common sense at last made its voice heard above the clamor of tearing heartbeats and unsteady breathing.

Maggie slid out of his arms and unconsciously ran the back of her hand across her tender mouth. She looked at him with reproach in her heart. "You have a rotten habit of keeping me off balance, do you know that?"

"You have the most beautiful breasts I've ever had the pleasure of—"

"Stop that! Do you have to be such an awful cad?"

Mick laughed. "A cad? A *cad*? You didn't expect me to get nice all of a sudden, did you? After being rotten has gotten me this far?"

Maggie stood up hastily and brushed off her jumpsuit as though she had just accumulated a month's worth of dust on the material. Mick lazed to his feet, too, and they stood for a moment, eyeing each other. Mick looked relaxed and amused. Maggie remained on guard.

"Afraid still?" he asked.

"Not of you," Maggie whispered, and it was true. There was someone else to be cautious about—the stranger who lived inside herself.

Whether he understood her feelings or not, Maggie wasn't sure. But Mick leaned forward cautiously and gave her a polite peck on the forehead. "Good night, Miss Margaret," he said simply.

"Good night?"

"Yes, good night. That's the proper thing to say according to all the etiquette books, right?"

"Yes, but—"

"You look surprised."

Maggie controlled herself. "Surprised? Why—I—you—"

He chucked her under the chin. "I can be a perfect gentleman as much as the next guy. 'Night, Maggie. Sweet dreams."

Five

Blast him,'' Maggie muttered when she was alone in her room. "He's got me *wishing* for kisses now! I'm supposed to fall into his arms and prove I'm a woman!''

She glared at herself in the mirror. "You are,'' she muttered at last.

But not the kind of woman the likes of Mick Spiderelli was accustomed to. He probably liked his females long on Kama Sutra and short on scruples. She wasn't going to stoop to his level.

"I'm too much of a lady for that!''

But Maggie didn't sleep for hours. She climbed into bed and tossed and grumbled and listened to the rain on the roof until nearly dawn. Then the villa was quiet, the sun began to lighten the edges of the window, and Maggie fell deeply asleep.

When she woke, she smelled coffee and thought lazily that she'd been dreaming—perhaps everything had been a dream. A shaft of sunlight pierced the curtains on her windows, and the gentle movement of breeze-rustled palms created eddies of light on the bed. When a dazzle of sunshine caught her across the eyes, Maggie remembered that she hadn't been dreaming. Mick was in her house. He'd connived his way into the villa, and now into her imagination, too. He played games, turning her conscious brain against her body. A part of her wanted to finish those games. She wanted to touch him, to feel the muscle beneath his brown skin and learn the secret behind that quick laugh and knowing grin of his.

The telephone woke her from that fleeting fantasy. Automatically, Maggie checked her bedside clock to note the time. Her office had orders to telephone at precisely the same hour every day. Relieved to learn that it was ten on the dot, she reached for the receiver.

"Yes?"

It was a representative from the newspaper syndicate on the line, purely a business call to inform Maggie that two more newspapers had picked up her column for their Sunday editions. Also, said the young woman, they needed some copy concerning how and where to send letters to Dear Miss Margaret. Maggie sat up in the bed, pulled a notebook from the drawer in the night table and braced it on her knees.

She was briskly reading off her notes when she heard a tapping at her door.

Mick didn't bother to wait for an answer, but turned the handle and came right into her room balancing a tray and looking uncommonly cheerful. Maggie's voice faltered on the telephone, but she quickly regained her composure and finished delivering the information.

"That's all?" she asked the representative.

"Yes, ma'am," said her caller. "We'll send your check to your accountant, as usual?"

"Yes," said Maggie. "Thank you for calling. Good-bye."

She cradled the telephone.

Mick set the tray on the night table. "Good morning, sleepyhead! Are you going to waste this whole beautiful day in bed?"

Maggie clutched the bedclothes against herself. "What do you think you're doing?"

"Bringing you breakfast, milady." With a flourish, Mick shook out an embroidered napkin. "I heard you answer the phone, so I brought you something to start the day right. Here, tuck this under your lovely chin and I'll pour you some coffee. Sugar? Cream?"

"Black," Maggie said flatly, eyeing him with suspicion.

Her phone call had reminded Maggie that she was still in charge of at least one part of her life. She accepted the napkin from Mick and turned her attention to the food he'd brought. The tray was loaded with a huge breakfast complete with silver toast rack, fine china and crystal jam pot. She couldn't help noticing that Mick looked just as appetizing, freshly shaved and smelling like he'd just come from a revitalizing dip in the ocean.

He bowed like a devoted butler and handed her a china cup into which he then poured a fragrant stream of hot coffee from a silver pot. When she had taken the cup from his hand, he marched to the window and threw open the curtains. Instantly, the room was bathed in glorious sunlight, illuminating Mick in all his physical splendor. He had on a clean pair of denim shorts that showed off his powerful long legs, and a faded black T-shirt that was skintight across his shoulders. He unfastened the window and swung it open so that a gust of storm-fresh air suddenly blew into the room. It carried a scent to Maggie, faintly salty and masculine, that she recognized as Mick's. As he returned to the bed, bent over the tray and poured himself a cup of coffee from the pot, she was momentarily mesmerized by the play of muscle and sinew in his body. He stood so close beside her that she could have reached out and touched his face, slipping her fingertips down the strong column of his throat, down his shoulder, across the beautiful contour of his back. The temptation to do just that, in fact, nearly overcame her.

Mick set the pot back down onto the tray, thoroughly unaware of the reaction he'd provoked. "The rest of us have been up for hours. Your housekeeper turned up a short while ago. She's doing last night's dishes and listening to the radio, and her husband just took the kids down the beach to buy fruit. I went out to check my boat and got some clothes for me and Spider—"

"She's listening to the radio? You mean the generator's fixed?"

"Sure," said Mick. He kicked off his shoes and stretched out on the foot of the bed, contentedly cradling his cup and looking her straight in the eye. "I did it myself."

Clearly, there was no end to the man's talent, nor his willingness to put it to use. "I see," she said at last. "It seems I am in the position of thanking you again."

He shrugged and drank deeply from his cup. "No problem," he replied, smiling as winsomely as an Italian leprechaun. "Believe me, I'll exact a payment."

Maggie sipped her coffee and arched her brows, hoping she looked serene. "What kind of payment?"

His grin broadened, reflecting pure mischief, and he allowed his gaze to stray down the outline of her body beneath the bedclothes in a can't-you-guess expression. But Maggie's face must have changed, because he laughed. He said, "No, I haven't come to deflower the princess in her bower! I wanted to see how you looked this morning, Miss Margaret. That's payment enough."

Tartly, she said, "I'm fine this morning, thank you very much. I don't get hangovers, if that's what you're hoping."

"You didn't drink enough champagne to give a hangover to a hummingbird," he retorted. "No, I meant your outfit. I thought I might catch you sleeping in the buff. Instead, you look like something out of a Victorian picture book. I should have known. Doesn't all that lace choke you during the night?"

Maggie managed a disdainful look, but her fingers strayed automatically to the prim collar of her nightgown. "I don't buy my lingerie at Fredericks' of Hollywood, Mr. Spiderelli. I'm sorry to disappoint you."

"I'm not disappointed," he said, and this time his voice was suddenly half an octave lower. The sound of it caused Maggie's heart to trip and accelerate. But when Mick allowed his gaze to stray from her face down the lace-covered curve of her breast, the look that crept into his eyes was not quite admiring. In fact, he looked almost bored for a moment. Contentedly, he drank from his coffee cup.

Pride welled up inside Maggie and stiffened her spine. So he didn't find her desirable after all.

She set her cup back on the tray with a sharp rap. "Thank you for bringing me my breakfast," she said briskly. "If you run along now, I'll get dressed." She threw back the bedclothes to demonstrate she had no intention of continuing the interview.

"It's my breakfast, too," Mick said ignoring her dismissal. He sat up and folded his long legs, Indian style. Reaching past her for the tray, he plucked a piece of toast from the rack. "Look at this! The crusts cut off and everything. You rich and powerful folks must not like curly hair. Do you prefer marmalade or butter?"

"Listen," Maggie began sternly, holding the coverlet tight against her stomach to quell its churning. "I'm not accus-

tomed to sharing my bedroom *or* my breakfast with anyone, Mr. Spiderelli. I like to get up and get dressed at my
own pace, so if you'd—''

"Tut, tut," he said. "Didn't we get up on the wrong side
of the bed this morning!"

"I haven't the faintest notion which side of the bed *you*
got up on," Maggie began, "but I'm not a morning person
to begin with and—"

"Come on," he protested, slathering orange marmalade
over every square inch of the toast. "You don't have to be
Emily Post every waking minute, do you? Just relax. It's a
beautiful morning!" He gestured with his toast, dribbling
crumbs on the coverlet but paying that no mind. "Look at
that sunshine! This is no day to be so uptight."

"I'm not uptight."

"Yes, you are."

"I am not!"

"You're so tight I could play 'Ave Maria' on you! Here,
have some toast."

Maggie caught the toast just as Mick tossed it her way, but
she bobbled the catch and smooshed sticky marmalade between her fingers. "Oh, murder," she muttered, eyeing the
mess with distaste.

"See? That's a good example of uptightness," Mick remarked, helping himself to another piece. "Now, a real
woman would just loll back on those pretty pillows and lick
her fingers. But you'll probably head straight for the bathroom sink, right?"

Maggie had been about to do exactly as he predicted. She
stopped herself, however, realizing that in order to get to the
bathroom, she was going to have to expose herself and her
nightgown to Mick's quick observation. No doubt he'd have
a field day with her prim and proper choice of nightwear.
Not only did her nightgown cover her throat clear up to her
chin, but the voluminous pink fabric also fell to her ankles.

No, she didn't want to give him more opportunity for making fun of her.

Suddenly it was darned important to her that Mick Spiderelli change his opinion of Miss Margaret Kincaid.

Giving him a contrary look, Maggie therefore chose to lick the marmalade from her fingers. Thank heaven he didn't know how stirred up she felt inside! The sweetened fruit melted deliciously on her tongue, and Maggie lay back against her pillows to finish the job.

Mick felt a queer sensation expand in his chest as he watched her little kitten's tongue fastidiously clean every dribble of sweet jam from her slender fingers. He'd never met such a persnickety woman—a woman so refined, so strict with herself, so utterly unapproachable. And yet he *wanted* to approach her. He wanted to wrap his arms around her slim little body, to inhale the subtle female perfume that seemed to waft in the air wherever she went, to nuzzle her silky hair and coax the warmth out of that small, luscious mouth again. The thought of trying sent Mick's blood coursing.

But he went on consuming his toast, trying to slow down the unbidden rush of excitement that surged within him. Why did this woman—of all women in the world—affect him so intensely? In bed last night, he'd ached for hours, his head filled with images of her, his body yearning as it hadn't done in years. With Maggie, he felt like a kid again—full of lust and longing. Watching her sitting there against the ruffled pillows, her hair tumbled from sleeping and her softcolored eyes still not quite wide awake, Mick felt ready to burst. He wanted to take that lacy little nightgown of hers and rip it with his bare hands.

Daintily, she finished her wedge of toast and reached to the breakfast tray for a dish of melon balls. She took it into her lap and with a small silver spoon, began to eat the fruit.

The sight of those moist, colorful bits of melon disappearing down her throat nearly tore a groan from Mick.

Knowing he sounded far from normal, he said, "You look beautiful this morning, Miss Margaret."

She swallowed a bit of melon and looked at him. Rather than reacting with a cool look or a swift down-turning of her mouth, Maggie took the unexpected compliment with only a slight widening of her soft gray eyes.

"You're supposed to say thank you," he chided, trying to keep the rasp out of his voice. "At least, that's what I read in Dear Miss Margaret."

"Thank you," she whispered.

Curiosity gnawed so hard that Mick finally had to ask. "Why is it so difficult?" he said.

"What do you mean?"

"No matter how I say it, you can hardly accept a compliment from me. What's the matter? Don't I phrase them right?"

"No," she said at once. She toyed with the remaining fruit in her dish as if she'd suddenly forgotten she was hungry. "I—It's just that I have the feeling you say those things to manipulate me."

"To—?" Mick laughed. "My dear Miss Margaret, what kind of a heel do you think I am?"

"Not a heel," she said. "Just different. You're not like anyone I've ever been around before."

Mick watched her for a moment, a beautiful, untouchable woman radiant in the glow of molten sunlight. "It's a shame we're such different kinds of people," he said.

She went on looking at him steadily, her knees drawn up like a little girl. "What kind of person are you?"

"Last night I behaved like a perfect gentleman. But right now," said Mick, "I want to climb into that soft bed of yours, Miss Margaret, and..." He couldn't finish the sentence. Erotic thoughts overwhelmed him, and he knew any more words would scare Maggie. She could back into her shell faster than any turtle on earth.

But her voice was softly insistent. "And what?"

Grimly, Mick looked away and shook his head. "No. Never mind. You're not a morning person, anyway, are you?"

A pink flush crept up her throat, coloring her cheeks a charming rose. "I could be," she said. "On the right morning."

That surprised him. But what came next was even more of a jolt. Mick looked around at her, and for a split second, Maggie didn't move. She went on gazing at him speculatively, but Mick felt she wasn't really seeing him entirely. She was battling herself, fighting an impulse. Unsteadily, she put the fruit dish back on the tray.

Then she came at him like a cat—slowly, but lithe and purposeful—without a wasted motion. Mick held his breath, prepared for her to stop, to have second thoughts. But she wound her slender arms around his shoulders, and in the next moment her soft breasts were pressing gently against his chest. The effect was electric. Instantly, Mick felt his every nerve come alive. She was in his arms! Willingly! Impetuously! He knotted his hands in the silky fabric of her nightgown, half in an effort to control himself. Her hair glinted in the sunlight. Her gentle perfume enveloped him. She was soft. She was intoxicating.

And she was trembling. "I don't know why you do this to me," she whispered.

"I'm not doing a thing this time."

"Yes, you are. You're muddling me up inside. You make me confused about myself." In a tortured whisper, she said, "I'm scared to death, but I—I just want to find out."

Then she kissed him. Her lips were sweet. She eased her fingers through his hair and pressed her mouth to his, opening, searching, staking her tentative claim.

She surprised the hell out of him. Her kiss was melting, almost tender. For an instant Mick didn't react. Then suddenly he was struggling with self-control. It unraveled inside him, coming apart in hundreds of liquid threads that teased his nerve endings.

He gripped Maggie's shoulders hard. He kissed her back, pouring every ounce of lust he'd ever felt for her into those ten seconds of bliss. He wanted to push her down onto the bed, to open her body and take her swiftly. Years had passed since he'd felt desire this immense. It almost hurt inside, those long-dormant feelings.

She ended the kiss gradually, and when it was over, Maggie clung to him, her eyes still closed. She sighed—in relief, perhaps. But her fingers were tight on his shirt. And the sight of her small face tipped up to his—softened in surrender, flushed with desire—caused the one part of Mick's body that he couldn't control to come fully alive. Whether she felt it or not, he couldn't be sure. She seemed to be still locked in battle with herself.

"Oh, Mick," Maggie whispered. "I'm lost."

"No, you're not. You're right here."

"Yes, here with you and wishing we could just—oh, darn it! I don't know what to do."

But Mick knew exactly what came next. He wanted to be naked with her, get skin to skin with her soft flesh and to-hell-with-the-consequences. He struggled with his shirt, then yanked it over his head in one violent motion. "This gentlemanly garbage is for the birds!"

Maggie gasped, and her eyes flew open. Mick threw his shirt to the floor, determined to put an end to the cat-and-mouse game. He gripped her, pulling Maggie against his hard frame to let her feel how aroused he was.

"Maggie," he said, nearly choking on his own seething desire. "Touch me. Now. Feel my heart beating?"

She obeyed, putting her shaking fingers against his throat. The touch turned to a caress, and she smiled. It was as though the sun had risen in her face, so radiant were her eyes. "Yes, I feel it."

"Do you understand?" Mick felt like shaking her. His fingers bit into her silky flesh. "Do you know what it means?"

"Yes. You—it means you like me, after all. A little bit, at least."

"*Like* you? Darling innocent, it means I want you. I want to take you, make you mine. And in a minute, I won't be able to stop."

"I don't want you to stop," she whispered, her hands playing along the hard contours of his chest. Recklessly, she tilted her mouth up to his, and he saw everything in her face—fear, yes, but excitement, too. And trust. Somewhere along the line, she had started to trust him.

With her tantalizingly soft mouth curved into a shy smile, all she said was one word. "Let's."

Mick was only human. He fought himself for a moment longer, but he couldn't hold back. He kissed her, delving into her mouth and crushing her body against his. He could feel the heat of her breasts through the modest nightgown, her slender legs quivering in anticipation. That damned nightgown! Fumbling, he found the pearly buttons at the back of her neck. One popped and skittered somewhere on the floor, and Mick thought she'd pull away, fearing his assault. But she didn't. The poor innocent hadn't any clue how ferocious his desire was.

Don't scare her, Mick commanded himself. With the fabric clenched in his hands, he made one last stab at being noble. "Are you sure?" His voice was hardly more than a rasp.

"Yes." Then her eyes fluttered open, suddenly clouded with uncertainty. "But—the children?"

GET YOUR GIFTS FROM SILHOUETTE®
ABSOLUTELY FREE!

Mail this card today!

PLACE
JOKER
STICKER
HERE

PLAY THIS CARD RIGHT!

YES! Please send me my four Silhouette Desire® novels FREE along with my free Digital Clock/Calendar and free mystery gift as explained on the opposite page.

225 CIL JAYR

NAME _____
(PLEASE PRINT)

ADDRESS _____ APT. _____

CITY _____

STATE _____ ZIP CODE _____

Prices subject to change. Offer limited to one per household and not valid to current Desire subscribers.

SILHOUETTE BOOKS
"NO RISK" GUARANTEE

- There's no obligation to buy—and the free books remain yours to keep.

- Unless you tell us otherwise, every month we'll send you six more books, months before they appear in stores.

- You may end your subscription anytime—just write and let us know, or return the shipment to us—at our cost.

IT'S NO JOKE!

MAIL THE POSTPAID CARD AND GET FREE GIFTS AND $10.00 WORTH OF SILHOUETTE® NOVELS — *FREE!*

"They're gone for the morning. We're alone."

Maggie cupped his ribs, her fingers sliding along his flesh with agonizing gentleness. The points of her breasts rubbed deliciously against his chest, and she arched against his arousal, probably not even realizing how erotic her slightest movement felt. "The door," she whispered, her lips touching his. "We'd better lock it."

"The hell with that," Mick growled. "I'm not leaving this bed for anything."

He crowded her back against the headboard and tore the nightgown from her without apology. Maggie's body was more beautiful than he'd imagined. She was smooth, but curving. Not boy-sleek, but womanly in the most delicate sense; she looked so lovely and vulnerable that Mick's throat began to ache. Her white skin, translucent as shell, was the perfect backdrop for the sauciest, rosiest pair of nipples Mick had ever seen.

"You're an angel," he said.

She helped him undress. But when he was naked, Maggie began to tremble all over again. "I'm not—I haven't had much experience at this."

"Touch me," he said, taking her hand. "Like this."

She did as he commanded.

"You see?" he said. "How much I want you?"

"Yes, but—" She shrank back, suddenly filled with uncertainty.

"Are you worried? Isn't this a safe time?"

"Yes, it's safe. I'm just— It's not that at all." Maggie struggled with the words. She squeezed her eyes closed. "What if I can't please you?"

Mick laughed, his heart filling with joy and the pleasure to come. He touched her face. "You don't get the point, love."

Mick whipped back the sheets and coverlet and carefully laid Maggie in the middle of the uncluttered bed. Her hair spilled out like dark, fragrant ribbons, and her slim legs parted when he insistently prodded with his knee. She lay quietly, looking up at him with a mixture of trust and anxiety, her hands resting on his upper arms. Mick stared down at her hungrily. Here was a challenge of the sweetest kind— to lead a lovely woman into the realms of physical pleasure while slaking his own raging thirst at the same time. And he wanted every inch of her—every breath and shiver. He wanted to see her face when she cried out. He wanted to feel her convulse around him when he sank inside her body. He wanted everything.

"Oh, dear," Maggie said laughingly as she finally caught sight of his lusty expression.

Restraint, Mick lectured himself. This was no time for rushing anything. He cupped Maggie's face between his palms and smiling, kissed her mouth, knowing he'd better calm down before he frightened her with his uninhibited impulses. Gently, he touched his lips to her cheek, her delicate eyelids, her temples. Against her mouth once more, he murmured, "I won't do anything you don't want. Trust me?"

"Yes," she whispered.

He began gently, first exploring her throat, her earlobes until he could feel Maggie's limbs relax a little against his own. After a moment, she even sighed at the sensations his nibbling lips evoked.

Then he started towards her breast, but remembered his promise. "May I?"

She nodded unsteadily, and when his mouth skimmed her flesh, she gasped a soft breath. He grew bolder at once and suckled her—too fast, perhaps. Maggie writhed beneath him.

"Oho, my beauty, not so fast!" Pretending she had struggled to escape, Mick pinned her to the bed. Maggie gave a breathless huff of laughter, and when he looked up, her eyes were brimful with something new—curiosity, he thought.

She seized his hair gently, smiling. "Get down to business, friend. Or the whole morning will be gone before you know it."

She was warming to the game. The poor unfortunate had never enjoyed herself with a man! The uncertainty in her eyes showed how she hung torn between shyness and desire. Suddenly Mick wanted that more than his own release. With renewed purpose, he caressed her, kissed her, nibbled her, reveling in the softness of her skin, the swiftness of her heartbeat. And Maggie responded. When his teeth lingered on her nipple, she clutched his head and pulled him closer. When he smoothed his hand down her body and traced the pattern of dancing sunlight on the curve of her stomach, watching her face, she reacted with short gasps. Each spiral of the pattern went lower until he brushed the tangle of curls that seemed to draw his fingertips. As if he'd asked permission, she said, "Touch me now."

"You're not still scared?"

"Of me," she whispered. "Not you. Yes, touch me. Everywhere."

He drew imaginary images on her sun-washed thighs and signed his handiwork with kisses. Then he pressed her open and found a more delicious target. He teased her with his tongue, exploiting every nuance of his experience until she seized handfuls of the sheet beneath her and shuddered with a low cry.

Maggie didn't recognize herself. Mick was doing wonderful things to her, terrible, marvelous things, and she could only cry out for more. He explored her most vulnerable spots, smoothed her skin with his hands, warmed her body with his breath. Maggie arched to meet his every caress, overwhelmed with delight. He laughed, coaxing her to let down her walls of control until Maggie laughed breathlessly with him.

There was a fire inside her, something very new, and Mick had kindled it. She wanted him, this tough, wild demon, who'd burst into her life. She wanted him inside her, firing her blood with his, sharing his power. He had led her to the brink of a sunrise, and Maggie was suddenly afraid to plunge over the horizon's edge without him.

"Mick!"

"Soon, love."

But unable to stand the tension any longer, Maggie guided him herself.

Mick loomed over her for an instant, larger than life in that shimmering sunlight, bone and muscle and supple sinew coupled to a spirit more powerful than any man she'd known. Carved on his face was a look of wild hungry pleasure, and when he found her warmest spot and pressed inside, he made a sound—half in triumph and half a tortured growl—that shook Maggie's soul. He sheathed himself inside her body, going so deeply she dared not breathe until he was locked within her.

Mick caught his deeply she dared not breathe until he was locked within her.

Mick caught his breath so suddenly that Maggie mistook it for a tight, inexplicable sob. He had closed his eyes and for a long moment seemed locked in a memory. Then, slowly, he relaxed, his body finding comfort in hers. Without thinking, Maggie wrapped her arms around him.

"Mick?"

"I'd forgotten," he murmured, his lips caressing her ear. "How beautiful this could be."

It *was* beautiful, Maggie realized in a flash of astonishment. And it was Mick who had made the difference. She trusted him, enjoyed him, wanted to know more about him.

Something deep inside him cried out to her, like a child's call in the night.

And with Mick she could be free. There was no awkwardness, no frustration. He cared as much for her pleasure as his own. Maggie felt her excitement soar to a new height as that understanding blossomed in her mind.

"Now, Mick," she urged, not wanting to enjoy the inevitable release of building tension alone.

He needed no more encouragement. Drawing her hair back from her face, Mick could see how close she was, how intensely she fought to hold back her own fulfillment. His heart swelled with a sweet pressure. Pinning her against the bed, Mick rocked between her slender thighs, surging gently at first, then with increasing power until he drove her almost savagely over the edge. With a single, passionate thrust, they were one, sharing in that instant a burst of incandescence as fiery as the rising sun. It flashed around them, pulsing, then diminished slowly in a starry, all-consuming shower of light.

Maggie held him, enveloping Mick with her arms and pulling him back to earth. And if she cried out in that moment, Mick smothered the sound with his mouth, perhaps partly to stifle his own rasp of release. His kiss was hard, but soon turned gentle as her involuntary sounds ceased.

The timeless moment slid by. They lay quietly, eyes closed, to savor the slow return of reality. Maggie let the warmth of his body and the still-flickering currents of passion soothe her back into a drowsy doze.

At last Mick rolled away, untangling her sleepy arms from around his neck. Alone, he sat up. He was dazed.

How easy it had been. Mick glanced over his shoulder at Maggie's serene face, relaxed but not quite asleep. She looked more beautiful than when she was awake. She was too wary when awake. But sleepy and satisfied—she looked so tranquil and lovely that it made his chest ache.

Her tangled hair lay under his hand, and for an instant, he coiled a ribbon of it around his finger remembering the softness of another woman's hair, the sweet music of her cries when he had made love to her. The memories swept up quickly and caught him off guard, memories he thought he'd buried very well.

"Mick?" Maggie's murmur was soft, and her feather-light touch on his back was gentle. "What's wrong?"

"Nothing," he said at once.

But he'd felt remorse begin to stir. He closed his eyes to the feeling, but there was no stopping it.

Maggie sat up. "Yes, there is something the matter. I've known it from the start. What is it?"

He pasted a grin back on his face and turned to her, gathering Maggie in a swift embrace. He even managed a pretty fair imitation of a laugh. "Nothing's the matter. I was just thinking how wonderful you are."

She smiled doubtfully.

"What's this?" he demanded, feigning amusement. "Second thoughts?"

"No, not that. You—I thought you withdrew just now."

"It's your imagination." He kissed her mouth again and brushed his lips back and forth before asking, "How about a swim? Some sun on the beach? We've only started this day, you know."

Her eyes widened in surprise, and Mick laughed. "Nothing can top that performance, eh? Well, you'd better think again, Miss Margaret. Get into your swim suit, all right? We've got things to do today."

She made no move to hold him back, and Mick got up quickly and found his clothes. With Maggie watching in reserved silence, he got into his shorts, then bent over her one last time for a kiss. She watched his eyes with a disconcertingly knowledgeable look, and Mick let himself out into the hall quickly. Damn the woman! She saw too much!

For Maggie, the magic of the morning evaporated when the door clicked shut behind him, leaving her alone to decide what had gone wrong.

"My God," she murmured. She buried her face in her pillow and held very still. Had she misjudged him? Made a terrible mistake?

Cringing, she could imagine Mick strolling up into the kitchen in a satisfied male euphoria to open a bottle of beer. The conquering hero had gone for the gusto, vanquished his princess, and now needed some refreshment.

"What did you expect?" she muttered to herself. "Champagne and strawberries and tickets to tonight's opera?"

Her body had betrayed her. She had known better than to get involved with a tough customer like Brooklyn's own Mick Spiderelli. But after making love with him, Maggie felt as if she was floating. The muscles of her limbs weren't exhausted, but felt languorous and wonderfully refreshed instead. Could something that left her so satisfied be so terrible?

She stared down at the rumpled bed, the sheets ripped out from beneath the mattress, the pillows strewn every which way. Who had that woman been—the one who tore the bed apart making such wild love? And with a perfect stranger, no less? Certainly not Mary Margaret Kincaid?

Laughingly, Maggie groaned, wondering did she wish to snatch back the last hour of her life? No, the lazy satisfaction she felt couldn't possibly be bad. She stretched like a cat and smiled.

The telephone interrupted her thoughts, and Maggie reached once again for the receiver. She didn't think. Pulling the covers up and snuggling comfortably against the pillow that still smelled ever so slightly of the man who'd just left, Maggie answered the call.

"Hello?"

Silence, at first, broken only by the crackle of long-distance static. Then a sigh. "Maggie."

She sat up at the sound of the voice. Her blood seemed to turn to ice water. Like a fool, she had answered the telephone without thinking.

"You're there, aren't you?"

Maggie released an unsteady breath. "Ben."

Ben Bratton chuckled smoothly. "Well, at least you still recognize the sound of my voice, honey."

Maggie marshaled her emotions. "What do you want?"

"You already know that, honey. I'm calling to talk to my man."

"What man?"

"The fellow I sent looking for you. I had a hunch you'd run to that rundown heap of rocks on the ocean, so that's the first place he was supposed to look. And Elizabeth is there, too, I understand."

Maggie's heart began to thump crazily. "Ben, what are you talking about? You—you sent him?"

"Yes, indeed. Hasn't he told you yet? Why, he must be following my orders more carefully than I expected. He's got a mind of his own, hasn't he?"

"Damn you, Ben—"

"Now, now, honey, certainly you understood how serious I am about this. I want to share the responsibility with you. A child needs a father. I'm the best man for that job! You just put yourself into the hands of my most charming employee and he'll see that you get here to my place in Baltimore in no time. It's—"

"I'm not going anywhere near you, Ben. I don't care who you've sent to kidnap me."

"Kidnap? Who ever said an ugly word like that?" Ben's voice hardened. "You don't have much choice, in any case. I'm looking at some charming pictures at this very moment, Maggie. Very charming. But I don't suppose everyone shares my taste in photography. How about if you get yourself and our daughter up here in three days or I'll make sure every newspaper that syndicates Dear Miss Margaret gets copies of these pictures.''

"Ben," Maggie said, summoning every shred of courage. "I don't care what you do to me. Elizabeth is worth more than—''

"Honey, newspapers aren't the only place I can send these photos. The principal at Elizabeth's school might be interested. Or some social workers in your neighborhood. Perhaps someone ought to decide if Maggie Kincaid is the kind of woman who ought to be allowed to raise a child alone. And how might Elizabeth react to a fuss like that?''

"Damn you," Maggie whispered.

Ben laughed. "Oh, honey, let's not hold a grudge. We've got a long life together, raising our child. Pack your bag and let our friend bring you home, all right? Maggie? Maggie, are you there?''

Maggie didn't answer. She sat for a time listening to Ben's distant voice, and then she gently put the receiver back in place. Like a sleepwalker, she got out of bed.

She dressed quickly. Swimsuit, jeans, sweater, sandals. Passport, money, and wallet went into a canvas beach bag. She pushed through her daughter's belongings methodically, trying to hold on to her composure with every ounce of strength. Clothes, shoes, Kangaroy. If she panicked now, she'd lose Elizabeth.

She avoided going up through the house toward the kitchen and Mick. Instead, Maggie let herself out the window of her room. With the beach bag dangling from her shoulder, she edged along the wall of the battlements. The sun had warmed the stone, and it felt good to press her cool face to the sandy surface for a moment. When she drew back, Maggie realized she had left a splotch of wetness on the stone. With a dull kind of surprise, she realized she was crying.

She dashed the tears from her face and climbed across the battlements to the terrace. Silently, she dropped to the floor, then stole down the stairway to the beach.

Half a mile up the beach she found Elizabeth in the company of Rico, the housekeeper's husband, and little Spider. They were strolling along pitching rocks into the ocean.

Maggie took Elizabeth's hand. "Come along, darling, let's take a walk."

"With Spider, too?" Elizabeth asked.

"No, just us. Rico, we'll catch up with you in a while. All right? Spider—"

The boy looked up at Maggie with Mick's black eyes—dark, sparkling, and piercing enough to see through a woman's soul. "It's okay," he said, fully aware that something was very wrong and he had nothing to do with it whatsoever. At once, he began to pull back, to withdraw into himself. He looked at Elizabeth and shrugged. "See you later, Lizzie."

Elizabeth didn't understand the finality that Spider sensed. Happily, she couldn't stop talking as they hiked quickly down the beach toward the town. "Mama, we've had such a wonderful morning. The storm washed all kinds of junk up onto the beach."

"Junk," Maggie murmured, "yes."

The resort town lay four miles from the villa, and Maggie walked the distance as if chased by the devil himself. Elizabeth's energy flagged, and Maggie carried the girl piggyback. By lunchtime they arrived at the harbor. Maggie headed for the road to hire a taxi.

She had just started to mount the rickety wooden stairs to the street, when a voice hailed her.

"Why, if it isn't Mrs. Spiderelli!"

At the mere mention of that name, Maggie wheeled around like a cornered animal.

"Don't you remember me? I'm Peter Samson. We met yesterday before the storm. I see you found your daughter."

The elderly gentleman beamed at Elizabeth in a friendly way, blue eyes twinkling. He wore a lime-green shirt today with his signature ascot of white silk around his neck and his jaunty yachting cap set at a rakish angle on his head. "You two look exhausted! May I buy you some lunch?"

Maggie *was* tired. She let Elizabeth slide off her back but clasped her hand firmly. She mustered a smile. "Thank you, but not today—"

"I see. You're probably going on a picnic, right?" He bent down to address the child. "You must like picnics, young lady."

Elizabeth shyly smiled back at Peter Samson. "We had one last night," she said. "But not today. Mama says we're going away."

"Away?" Peter Samson straightened and looked at Maggie.

"Yes," she said. "We're on our way to the airport right now."

"Oh," said the gentleman. "Have they opened it already?"

"What?"

"The airport. It was damaged in the storm last night. I just came from there myself. I was supposed to pick up some guests and go for a cruise, but the storm ruined our plans. You did know about the airport, didn't you?"

"No," Maggie said, distractedly. The airport closed! She hadn't thought to call. Her first instinct had been to run. She needed more time to think, more time to plan what method she had to fight Ben with. Suddenly overpowered by too many worries, Maggie felt horribly dizzy. The ocean breeze was enough to sway her off balance.

Peter Samson caught her and steadied Maggie with both hands. "My dear!" he said.

Maggie tried not to cry. Not in front of Elizabeth! But with a distinctly weepy catch in her voice, she said, "I'm in a jam, Mr. Samson."

"Let me help," said the grandfatherly stranger. "My boat is tied up just down this way. Come aboard."

Six

———

Mick walked up the beach away from civilization, awash in memories he thought he'd buried within himself a long time ago. Funny how intimacy with other women hadn't affected him before, but suddenly he had to be alone. He climbed the rocks on the spit of island, which curved away from the villa, and stood watching the surf crash and spray, turning the air to sparkles. Inexorably, the tide began to pull each wave farther and farther back from the jagged rock so that more tumbled stones appeared through the sun-dazzled foam with every passing minute. The saltwater misted his face, the sun beat down on his shoulders, and Mick forgot about time for a while. He forgot about Maggie. Or tried to. The mental images of two women—both sweet and shy and painfully vulnerable—blurred in his head.

Perhaps an hour passed. Maybe two. Like the rock around him, rooted permanently in the earth as the tide retreating around it, the pain came to light slowly and soon lay bare in the sun. Making love with Maggie Kincaid had weakened his defenses, exposing the ache, the longing, soul-rendering grief he had never learned to accept. Mick made no effort to suppress the emotion as it rose within him. Months had passed since he'd last let himself remember.

He was still sitting on the rocks when Spider found him.

The boy clambered up as nimbly as a monkey, full of life and energy as always. "Dad!" he called, jumping barefoot from one foothold to another. "Whatcha' doin'?"

"Nothing," said Mick, but his words were too soft and the breeze snatched them away.

Spider took one look at his face and knew everything. "You been thinking about Mom?" he said.

Mick smiled. The boy was just as perceptive as his mother had been. "Some," he admitted, for they had never kept their feelings a secret from each other. He held out one hand. "Come here."

His son ignored the hand and slipped naturally onto Mick's lap instead and wrapped his sturdy arms around his father's neck. Mick held him hard and gave thanks the boy wasn't too grown up not to want his share of hugs and kisses. Contentedly, Spider clung and nuzzled his face close, and Mick put his nose against Spider's dark, wiry hair, willing the lump in his throat to go away. He should be happy with the reminder fate had graciously left behind. The boy was the only human being Mick had truly allowed inside his heart since Victoria's death.

"It's okay," Spider said. "I still miss her, too."

The lump didn't go away, but instead got harder and felt like a baseball. Mick knew he wasn't just suffering from grief anymore. He had wanted to keep his memories alive, at least; to see the woman he'd loved in his mind's eye at any given instant, like a series of finely painted portraits, full of light and color and all the things that best illustrated her character. But somehow Maggie Kincaid had caused the pictures of Victoria to fade and soften. The images were blurred. Mick couldn't simply shut his eyes and call into his imagination one of the many moments he'd hoped to preserve forever. Maggie intruded into all of them, it seemed, and Mick couldn't stop her.

Mick had always thought he could keep those memories pure. He'd promised Victoria. But he was failing.

"I liked this one better than the others," Spider said, at last.

"What?"

"She didn't tell me what to do or get all gushy, either. That lady from New York was the worst, but this one wasn't too bad."

"Who?" Mick asked, still trying to sort out the past from the present.

"Elizabeth's mom." Spider began to swing his legs nonchalantly. "She was the prettiest. And she was okay."

Mick grinned. "Was? You've written her off already?"

Spider narrowed his eyes. "What does that mean?"

"It means you've decided we're not seeing her anymore."

"We're not," Spider said, matter-of-factly.

"What?"

"She called."

Mick frowned. "Where did she call?"

"She telephoned the castle. She went to the town."

Without thinking, Mick gripped the boy's shoulders. "When? Why did she go?"

Spider shook off his father's tight grip. "I don't know. We met her on the beach, and she had a real funny look on her face. She took Elizabeth into the town, then called the lady in the kitchen to tell her she wasn't coming back. They're leaving."

"*When?*" Mick demanded.

"How should I know?," Spider shot back amiably. "A while ago. I looked for you but—"

Mick swore violently and got up, setting Spider abruptly on his feet. "We have to go after her, Spider. There's got to be a car. We can catch her at the airport. Come on. Let's—"

"Airport's closed."

Mick swung on the boy. "What?"

"The airport's closed. She went on a boat."

"Boat? What boat?" Mick grabbed him. "Dammit, tell me everything!"

Spider wasn't intimidated. He shrugged. "I didn't hear the whole story. She went on a boat, that's all. With the storybook guy."

"Storybook guy?"

"The one with the long hair."

"Samson," Mick breathed, releasing his son. "Damn!"

"What's wrong? Wasn't she supposed to go?"

"No," said Mick. "And specifically not with him."

"Why?"

Mick took the boy's hand. "If my guess is right, Mr. Samson was sent here to snatch the lady we were supposed to be protecting. Come on, kid. We've got to make some phone calls and pull up the anchor."

"We're going home?"

"Yes. To face one very unhappy client, I'm sure."

"Dad," Spider asked, "did you blow this case?"

"I'm afraid so, son. Very badly."

"Wow," said Spider. "I didn't think you ever made mistakes."

"We'll make it right," Mick vowed. "Let's saddle up our white horse and strap on the armor."

"Huh?"

"I'll explain later. C'mon."

* * *

"My God," said Maggie, when she understood.

"There's no sense getting hysterical," Peter Samson told her as the sun set that evening, the ocean turning azure, then violet around them. "We don't want to upset that pretty daughter of yours, do we? I suggest you relax and enjoy the cruise. My staff will provide you with any luxury you desire. We'll be in Baltimore in a matter of days."

"You can't do this!"

"My dear, I can indeed. I'll deliver you to your husband and—"

"Ben is not my husband!"

Graciously apologetic, Samson spread his hands. "Be that as it may, I have my orders. Once we arrive in Baltimore and I've been paid, you're free to handle this unfortunate affair as you see fit. Until then, Miss Kincaid, you're my guest."

"You mean, your prisoner."

"Let's not use that word around your daughter, all right? We don't want to traumatize such a nice little girl, do we?"

He was right, of course. Maggie was willing to endure nearly anything before she'd allow Elizabeth to guess something was so terribly wrong. She kept quiet after that and she submitted to being delivered into the hands of her enemy. She ate very little and slept not at all, it seemed. At night she lay on the bunk, holding Elizabeth in her arms and thinking—inexplicably—of Mick Spiderelli, whom she had left so very far behind.

In Baltimore, Ben Bratton met the boat at the harbor.

Ben was tall and slim and attractive in the style of a baby-faced movie star, all sharp chin and chiseled features, blond hair and a tan too professional and perfectly even to have been achieved by any means but a tanning salon. He dressed like a Wall Street banker, visited a manicurist regularly and bore all the outward mannerisms of an old-money dilettante. Only his blue eyes gave him away, for they darted like those of an insecure boy looking for signs of insincerity in the people he met. He could be dashing, but Maggie had seen him turn petulant if he didn't get the attention he expected. Assisting Maggie off Peter Samson's boat, however, he appeared to have decided to play it with charm.

"Honey!" he cried, all affection. Even his native Virginian drawl had been practiced to sound as though he'd just stepped off Daddy's plantation for a day or two. He kissed Maggie gallantly.

She wiped the kiss away with the back of her hand. "Don't," she warned, eyes narrow.

Ben chose to ignore her chilly response. He bent toward the little girl who stood just slightly behind her mother. "And this must be Elizabeth! My, aren't you the sweetest magnolia blossom! Do you know my name?"

"No," said Elizabeth, instinctively wary of such a friendly stranger.

"I'm—well, I suppose you can call me just plain Ben for now. Isn't that best, Maggie?"

"We'd like a cab," Maggie said at once, determinedly brisk. "Will you call one for us, please? Elizabeth and I haven't had a change of clothes in three days. We want to go home."

"Home! Why, Philly's an hour's train ride from here. I won't hear of it! Elizabeth, wouldn't you like to come to my house? I have a big bathtub with bubbles, a refrigerator full of soda pop and boxes and boxes of truffles. Doesn't that sound nice?"

"What are truffles?"

"What are—!" Ben clapped his forehead. "You poor, underprivileged child! They're chocolates. Chocolates so delicious, they're sinful. Nobody knows the truffles I've seen! Get it?" He chuckled at his own humor.

Elizabeth looked questioningly at her mother. Maggie tightened her hand around her daughter's and faced Ben firmly. "We want to go home, Ben."

Ben met Maggie's cold stare, and his smile stiffened around the edges. "Soon," he promised. "First we'll go to my place and talk. Mr. Samson, thank you for bringing these lovely ladies to me so promptly. Will you take a check?"

Later in his car, an expensive German sports model in which Elizabeth had to crouch in the space behind the front seat, Ben chatted pleasantly, pointing out the sights that might interest Elizabeth. Maggie kept silent, speaking only when she couldn't avoid it. She hadn't forgotten how glib and charming Ben could be. She *had* forgotten how smart he was, though. Caution had to be her watchword. Not until they arrived in his condominium and Elizabeth was safely out of earshot in the tub, did Maggie steel herself for a showdown.

"You can't behave like this, Ben. What you did was kidnapping, and I can press charges."

"But you'd want to avoid anything so unpleasant, honey, I'm sure. Can't we be civilized?"

"You dare ask that? After what you pulled?"

Ben led her into his living room. It was long and airy, with tall windows overlooking Chesapeake Bay. An interior decorator had been permitted to go wild with the room. The furniture was light, yet dramatic. Subtle watercolors hung on the walls. Ben seemed to expand with pride as soon as he entered the space. "Maggie" he said, "all I want is a chance to see my own child grow up. That isn't too much to ask, is it?"

"Sweet God above, don't feed me that line! What you want is money, pure and simple."

He paused in the act of pouring wine from a heavy crystal decanter and allowed his gaze to slip down her somewhat bedraggled but nevertheless attractive figure, with an appraising gleam. "You underestimate me, honey. You've lost a few pounds since I saw you last, haven't you? You look marvelous."

Stiff, Maggie said, "I have a proposition."

Ben raised his eyebrows delicately, smiling. "A proposition?"

"Purely a business one. I've had three days to plan it, and I think it's fair."

Ben took his glass of wine to the pastel-toned couch in front of the faux marble fireplace. He sat, crossed his legs, arranged the seam in his trousers and then smiled at her. "I'm all ears."

Maggie remained on her feet and left the glass of wine he'd poured for her on the sideboard. She hadn't changed clothes, her head was splitting from a tension headache, and her nerves had been rubbed raw by the long sail from the Caribbean to Baltimore. Still, she knew she had to hold together a little longer. She decided to take a lesson from Mick Spiderelli and be blunt.

"I offer you cash, Ben. It's clean and simple. I know my uncle paid you before, and I'm willing to pay again."

Ben raised his hand to stop her. "Honey, I've had cash before and I'm sorry to say that I've been unlucky with lump sums. I'd much rather have a steady income, you see, so—"

"I understand," Maggie interrupted. "I'm willing to give you a down payment now—all that I can spare from my savings. We'll arrange a schedule of future installments—I was thinking of three—and after an established period of time I will receive the photographs."

"Photographs?"

"Don't play games, Ben," Maggie snapped, her voice tightening. "You know exactly what I mean! I get the pictures *and* the negatives."

He went on smiling to himself and sipped his wine. "I almost forgot about those. Isn't that strange? I thought we could take care of this matter without dragging the photographs back into the picture." He paused, and chuckled. "Back into the picture—get it?"

"Dammit, Ben—"

"No, honey, I'm afraid that won't do." Patiently he said, "It's an awfully generous offer, but I think—"

"You think you'd get a sweeter deal if you managed Elizabeth's trust fund. You want to get your greedy mitts on her money!"

"Yes," said Ben.

"I've got eighty thousand dollars I can give you," Maggie said swiftly. "That's eighty in cash right now, and I'll find a way to give you more next year and the next."

Ben shook his head. Almost daintily, he used his index finger to wipe the wine from the rim of his glass. He licked his finger and looked at Maggie. "Eighty thousand isn't much. I got more the last time."

Maggie mustered her composure. She wanted to scream and throw things. She longed to snatch the fluted glass from Ben's hand and smash it against his marble hearth. She wanted to grind caviar into his exquisite rug and hurl wine against his watercolors. But she held on a little longer. "All right," she said, speaking calmly. "I could probably scrape together a hundred thousand."

"And another hundred thousand every year after that?"

She swallowed with difficulty. "I'm not a rich woman, Ben."

"I already know that, honey. Believe me, it was a shock to discover you weren't living off the Kincaid millions. Maybe it's time you asked Joseph for a loan?"

Gritting her teeth, she said, "Hell will freeze over before I ask him for anything."

"Tch, tch," said Ben. "Never say never."

"You're interested then?" Maggie asked, at last.

Ben stood up and strolled around the room. He must have known he looked handsome among his possessions; the dhurrie rug, the paintings, a collection of porcelains, a baby grand piano that Maggie knew he must have bought with a down payment taken from the money her uncle had paid him. If she knew Ben well enough, he had bought all his pretty things on time payments, confident he'd find a way to pay his debts when they all came due.

He sauntered to the piano, executed a smooth about-face and leaned an elbow on the polished wood. "Yes, I'm interested," he said.

Relief swept Maggie so intensely that she had to force herself to close the deal then and there. "A hundred thousand? That will keep you out of my life for a year?"

"For a year," he said. "Then I'll want more. I'm getting married, did I mention? I want to go on impressing her. She's a beautiful girl, smart as a whip and sexy as—well, she's rich, too, I might add."

"Congratulations," Maggie said tightly. "After the wedding, you'll have her money to play your games with."

"Yes, but I'll need you to float me until I can get my hooks into her assets. I'm giving a party Saturday night—to introduce myself to some of my fiancée's high-society friends. Can we get this money business cleared up before then? I'd like to hire a caterer."

"If I thought I was going to have you around my neck for the rest of my life, Ben, I don't think I'd go along with this scheme at all." Maggie took a deep breath. "But since you've got someone else to take over when I've run dry, I'll agree. I'll give you three payments and then—"

"Four," he said.

"Four!"

"That's what I want. Four installments and then you'll get the pictures. I'll even give you a few at a time, if you like.

I'll be sorry to part with them, of course, since I do enjoy taking them out of my drawer occasionally, but—"

Maggie cut him off. "I want some guarantees. How can I be sure you'll give up all the pictures?"

Ben smiled and lifted his glass in a mocking toast. "You'll just have to trust me, honey."

Seven

———

Five days after leaving the Kincaid villa in the Caribbean, Mick found himself doing his knight-in-shining-armor impression and crossing the drawbridge of another Kincaid bastion. The headquarters of Kincaid Publications was located in an ornate old building in the downtown section of Philadelphia. Mick and Spider entered the vaulted lobby hand in hand and rode a mahogany-paneled elevator up to the fifth floor where a solemn secretary took charge of Spider and ushered Mick into the inner sanctum of J. B. Kincaid.

J.B. was the kind of man who seemed to be six feet of bull-like strength and power. He spoke his mind, showed no mercy with his employees, fired subordinates at a moment's displeasure and could count far more enemies than friends. He smoked fat little cigars that chased away even the most determined ring-kissers. And he was one of the most successful of the old-style newspaper men in the nation.

But when he stood up and moved out from behind his mammoth teak desk, he stood barely five and a half feet tall. His head was bald, his eyes in a perpetual squint, and his clothing could only have been described as slovenly. He wore shiny trousers clinched by a belt lodged beneath a protruding, barrel-shaped belly, and his ink-stained white shirt showed perspiration stains both at the collar and around the meaty forearms where his sleeves were perpetually rolled. Mick suspected J.B. even had his shirts laundered without bothering to unroll the sleeves.

"Spiderelli," he said, facing Mick like a banty rooster. "You screwed up!"

"Yes sir, I did."

They shook hands anyway, then J.B. stepped back brusquely. He had the black stub of a cigar clamped between his teeth and he spoke around it effortlessly. "I heard you were the best in the business, and yet you couldn't keep tabs on one sunbathing woman and her five-year-old child. What's the matter? You one of those guys who doesn't like looking at half-naked women?"

"I enjoyed looking at your niece, as a matter of fact, J.B. She gave me the slip, that's all."

"I hired you because you once had a reputation for excellence. Now you're down on your luck and having a few bad years, but I took a chance on you—"

"And I blew it. I'm here to give you your money back," Mick snapped. "So simmer down."

"I don't want my money back! I want my niece pulled out of this jam! What happened? Did she figure out who you were?"

"No," said Mick. "She thought I was sent by Bratton, and she got scared. She took off after—when my back was turned."

"I've got news for you, son." J.B. snatched the cigar from his mouth and held it between a pudgy thumb and forefinger to point at Mick's chest. "She didn't just take off. Mary Margaret jumped into the arms of some other character—a man Bratton hired! They ended up in Baltimore a couple of days ago."

"She's in Baltimore now?"

"No, she brought the little girl back here yesterday. I've got men watching her place as well as Bratton's."

Mick put his hands into the pockets of his jeans and turned away. He paced to the window and looked out, not seeing the fogbound city beyond the window. On edge, he said, "J.B., things are a lot more complicated than you think."

The stocky newspaperman joined him at the window and eyed Mick sharply. "What do you mean?"

"Bratton is angling for custody of the daughter. She's got the trust fund he wants. I suspect he hankers for the social prestige his Kincaid connections could bring, too, but the bottom line is he's blackmailing your niece."

"Blackmail!" Angered, J.B. turned away and threw his smoldering cigar into an ashtray. He swore.

Mick had wrestled for days with the question of whether to tell J.B. everything he knew about Maggie's situation. Reasoning that his client was the one footing the bill, Mick had decided to come clean. He suspected Maggie would be furious if she knew what he was doing, but he also figured he'd never see her again. And if by chance he ran into her in the future, Mick had no doubt she'd hit him with the first heavy object she could reach anyway. She'd hate knowing she'd been lied to. Still, Mick had a code he followed. He had to act in the way that would help Maggie most whether she liked it or not.

So Mick told J.B. about her situation. He began at the beginning, pacing for a while, then sitting in a leather chair in front of the big desk. J. B. Kincaid had hired Mick only on a hunch that Maggie was in trouble. After five years in California, Ben Bratton had moved back to the East Coast and J.B. suspected the worst. He wanted Mick to keep an eye on Maggie, nothing more. Perching on the edge of his desk, J.B. listened to Mick's description of what had transpired.

At last J.B. grumbled, "I wondered if the pup would figure the trust fund angle someday. What else?"

Mick came close to telling J.B. about the pictures. But when he noticed two silver-framed photos on J.B.'s desk— one of Elizabeth smiling shyly and one of Maggie looking very young and pensive in her graduation cap and gown, he decided to keep news about Ben's bedroom shots out of the conversation. He owed Maggie that much privacy, and he didn't want J.B. to explode either.

So he simplified the story succinctly. "Bratton's demanding custody, and Maggie's afraid to fight him in court because of the negative publicity. She doesn't want to hurt you, but mostly she wants to protect Elizabeth from any kind of public ordeal."

"So what comes next?" J.B. asked.

Mick shook his head. "That's your decision. And Maggie's."

"I want your professional opinion. I paid for that much, didn't I?"

Mick reached into the breast pocket of his tweed jacket and withdrew a small envelope. He tossed it onto the desk beside the cigar which had fallen out of the ashtray and was slowly charring a black spot on the teak finish. He said, "I'm out of it. There's my advance money."

J.B.'s face turned purple. "Hell, boy, I'm giving you a chance to get back on your feet again! This is a case that will set you up all over again and—"

"I understand all the benefits of working for you, J.B.,"
Mick interrupted. "Believe me, your offer of money and
contacts with the law enforcement agencies is tempting. But
you lied to me, J.B. And I don't work for liars."

"I never lied to you!"

"The hell you didn't," Mick snapped, matching the older
man decibel for decibel. "You said your niece needed protection from an ex-husband. You told me Bratton intended
to kidnap the child, and that's why I took the case. You
didn't tell me you'd paid him to leave in the first place."

J.B.'s mouth opened and closed like that of a fish.

"You also didn't tell me that your niece hates your guts.
If I'd known what a messy affair this was, I'd have stayed
away even at the price you offered."

"And yet you're here," J.B. said shrewdly. "You could
have called on the phone and returned my check by mail.
Instead, you showed up here to—"

"I don't give a damn about you," Mick said. "I'm not on
your payroll anymore. But I'm thinking of offering my ser-
vices to the one who really needs them."

"Mary Margaret?"

"That's right. She needs help. Someone's got to get rid of
Bratton for her and make sure you don't go hire somebody
else to follow her around like she's your two-timing mistress."

J.B.'s eyes narrowed. "Why, you—"

Mick smiled coldly. "Yeah, I know about the woman in
your life, J.B. I also know you should have handled Maggie's trouble differently. You never should have gotten involved in the first place, at least not without her permission.
Maggie's not unreasonable, but you're treating her as
though she can't handle things alone. You're muscling in
without being asked, and that's the fastest way to spoil re-
lations with her completely."

"You talk like you care," J.B. remarked, cuttingly.

"I talk from experience," Mick shot back. "Maggie's a good woman. She's full of love and deserves a family that can reciprocate. The two of you should patch things up before it's too late."

"Too late?"

"Life's short," Mick said. And he got to his feet. "Someday you'll wake up and realize that time has run out before you could make things right. It's a hell of a feeling, J.B. You'd hate it just as much as I do."

Maggie lived in a town house just blocks from Kincaid Publications. It was a modest place, bought at a good price and renovated gradually so that it was now worth a substantial amount of money. She was proud of her home, for it represented her own hard work, and not a cent of inherited wealth.

Usually, she worked on her columns at home and once a week walked down to her uncle's headquarters to turn them in. On Friday morning, Maggie walked past the Kincaid Building on her way to the bank. She willed herself not to glance up at the windows of her uncle's office.

At the bank, she met with a nice man who had acted as a personal banker for most members of the Kincaid clan for a decade, and he helped her refinance the mortgage on her house to raise the money she needed to pay off Ben. Using a little Kincaid influence, she received the sum in three separate checks, then proceeded to two more banks in town to change the checks into cash. With her canvas shoulder bag packed with large bills, Maggie took a taxi home.

She paid the driver, got out of the car and stopped short on the sidewalk, stunned by whom she saw sitting on the stairs of her town house.

"Hi," said Spider, as casually as if they'd parted on the beach just ten minutes earlier. "Where's Elizabeth?"

Maggie stared at the boy as the two of them got to their feet, then she lifted her gaze to Mick, still unable to speak. He looked tall and strong, the perfect man around whom a frightened woman could throw her arms. She almost did.

But something chilly in his manner stopped her. "Hello, Maggie," he said. "We got your address at the newspaper office."

His voice was restrained, but he looked the same, just cleaned up a little. His hair was combed, his face was shaved. He wore jeans and a casual blue buttoned-down shirt with a tweed jacket, a well-worn outfit that wouldn't look out of place among the reporters hanging around a newspaper office. Again, Mick had managed to look as if he belonged in his surroundings. His face was different, though. More guarded. His dark eyes were completely devoid of the wicked gleam of fun that had burned so intensely before. Things were different now. He still exuded a magnetic kind of power, but he was deadly serious now.

She found her voice, at last. "What do you want?"

"Can we come in?"

"What for?"

"To talk," he said. "That's all."

His tone hit her like a slap in the face. Making love, it seemed, had cooled Mick's interest in her. In the nick of time, Maggie reined in her urge to touch him, to hug his broad shoulders and nestle against his chest. For an instant, she had been joyful at the sight of him. Clearly, however, Mick wanted nothing personal between them. Not anymore. He only wanted to talk.

Managing to sound just as cool, Maggie said, "I have enough troubles at the moment. I don't think we have anything left to say to each other."

Mick stepped in front of her, effectively blocking Maggie from escaping up the steps. "I'll be brief, I promise."

"Really, there's—"

"I only need five minutes, Maggie."

Even saying her name, he sounded distant. If she told him she was going to the nearest airport to fly to Timbuktu for the rest of her life, she doubted Mick would blink. Maggie tried to manufacture a flippant answer. But suddenly she didn't have the energy. He didn't care. Why should she? Their morning in bed must have been a big disappointment, for he acted as though she was nothing more than a woman he'd met once in passing on a vacation. Maggie dropped her gaze, afraid to let Mick see how bitterly sorry she was. And ashamed. She had let down her guard and slept with him, only to have her inadequacies thrown back in her face.

Without thinking, Maggie touched his son, the straightforward little boy she'd actually missed in the days they'd been apart. She stroked his curly hair. To the father, she said, "There's nothing to say. I've been to the bank already."

Mick moved then. He grabbed her wrist, perhaps harder than he realized. He pulled, forcing Maggie to look at him. Suddenly the world narrowed. The noise from the street, the buildings, the people moving around them all faded into a blur. The world included only the two of them, and in that instant Maggie felt the spark, the electric power of the man she'd lost control with once before.

"Why to the bank?" he demanded. "What's happened, Maggie?"

Afraid of the way her body responded when her mind knew the impossibilities, Maggie resisted and cried, "It's none of your business. Let me go—"

"I can help," Mick said—so softly that no one beyond five yards could have heard. But Maggie heard as clearly as if he'd shouted. "You don't have any reason to trust me," he went on, "but I'm the only person who knows the whole story. And I've got the right kind of experience."

"I don't need anyone's help," Maggie said swiftly, still shaken by her body's instinctive reaction to the man, "I'm handling this my own way. It's almost over."

Mick laughed roughly. "Love, it's just beginning. Are you paying him off? Is that why you've been to the bank?"

She threw up her head and glared. "Yes. I'm taking care of everything, so you can just go back to—to wherever you came from and I'll thank you to stay there! I'm alone in the world with my daughter, and I've got to learn to take care of us myself. You can go to hell for all I care!" She inhaled deeply, feeling terrible at once. Disengaging herself, she stepped back from Mick and added, unsteadily, "I'm sorry, Spider."

The boy blinked up at her and missed the point. He piped, "My dad says you're a good-manners lady."

Maggie swayed on her feet, holding desperately to the remnants of her composure. Tightly, she said, "Yes. Yes, I am. I'm not acting like one right now, though, am I?"

He shrugged. "You're pretty polite, even when you yell."

There was no answer to that, and suddenly Maggie was afraid she was going to burst into tears on a public street. Clumsy, she twisted away and her canvas bag slid off her shoulder. In an instant, it hit the sidewalk and fell open, scattering packets of money along the pavement.

"Wow," said Spider. "Look at all the loot!"

Mick swore under his breath. Then, "Pick it up, Spider. All of it. Inside, Maggie. Right now." He gripped her elbow hard and steered her up the stairs, releasing Maggie only when she had inserted her key in the lock and he went back to help Spider stuff all the cash back into the bag. Mick carried it up the stairs, and the two of them entered the house behind Maggie.

"Spider!" Elizabeth cried. "It *is* you!"

Mick closed the door behind them in time to see Maggie's daughter come catapulting down a set of carpeted stairs and crash joyously into Spider, who responded with equal excitement. The next few moments were filled with the chatter of children. They charged up the stairs, headed for Elizabeth's playroom. Spider threw his jacket over the banister and didn't look back.

Mechanically, Maggie dropped her keys on a table near the door and, as if emotionally drained, she leaned against the table with both hands and didn't turn around.

From the top of the stairs came another young woman, the one who had answered the door earlier that day. She had not invited them in when Mick called. She spotted Mick at once and warily descended the stairs, looking from Maggie to Mick and back again.

"Maggie?"

"Oh, Cilla." Maggie pulled herself together and even made an effort to smile. She began to unbutton her raincoat. "I'm back, obviously. Everything's all right?"

The woman glanced curiously at Mick. She was of medium height and slender, with a figure perfect for high-fashion. In fact, her suede miniskirt revealed a particularly exquisite pair of knees. A keen intelligence showed in her eyes, as well. In her hand she carried a pair of high-heeled shoes, and she came down the stairs in her stocking feet. She had more pronounced physical angles than Maggie, and looked as though her personality was equally prickly. "Yes, we're fine," she reported. "Elizabeth and I played some games and had a snack."

"Good. Thanks so much for baby-sitting. It was short notice, I know."

"No problem. You're sure everything's okay?"

"Yes, certainly. Cilla, this is Mick Spiderelli. My cousin, Priscilla Kincaid."

"Little Italy and I met earlier," Cilla cracked.

"Charmed," Mick murmured, matching her mocking tone.

Cilla looked him over with a critical eye. Brittlely, she asked, "Comfy out on the porch all morning?"

"Very much, thanks. You make a guy feel welcome."

"You're very lucky I didn't call the cops." She put on her shoes, threw him a last dirty look, then concentrated on Maggie. "Listen, I'll clear out if you want, Maggie, but if there's anything I can do—"

"Nothing really."

"I mean it." She jerked her head to indicate Mick. "If you want me to throw this character out, I'll do it."

"You and the Sixty-sixth Armored Cavalry!" Mick retorted.

"Sixty-six. Is that your IQ?" Cilla inquired sweetly. "Or your neck size?"

"This dragon lady is a relative of yours, Maggie?"

Cilla strode forward and jammed one finger into his chest. "Listen, chum, I don't know who you are, but if you think you can hurt my cousin, you'd better think again!"

"Hey, hey!" Mick threw up both hands in surrender. "I'm one of the good guys! Maggie, tell her I'm not as bad as I look."

"You look pretty bad," Cilla shot back. Then her mouth softened. "But I like that in a man. Is he really all right, Maggie?"

"He's not bad," Maggie said softly. "Now run along, Cilla, before you ruin Dear Miss Margaret's reputation entirely."

Cilla put on her coat, gave Maggie a kiss and left, but not before skewering Mick with a last warning look before she closed the door. "Watch your step. I'll break all your bones if you step out of line with my cousin," she promised.

"I like her," Mick said when he was alone with Maggie. "She's tough and she loves you."

Maggie sighed. "She's just taking care of me—like everyone else. Why does the world assume I'm helpless?"

She stalked into the living room, clearly angry judging by the stiff set of her shoulders. Mick followed slowly, gauging her mood.

"Maggie," he began.

"Don't," she said, cutting him off before he could get any further. "I don't want your offer of help. I don't need you here to supervise. I just want to be left alone to manage my own problems in a practical fashion. I can do it alone!"

"I'm sure you could," Mick said. "But there's no reason to try."

Mick reached for her. Her arms felt smooth and malleable in his hands, and he longed to slide his arms around her body and pull her closer still. He wanted to smell her hair, feel her legs against his. Maggie's warmth and softness had tormented Mick in his dreams, and now that she was so close he felt his blood beat faster.

"Your family wants to help," Mick told her gently, hoping to coax a smile from her angelic lips. "They love you, and they don't want you to go through this ordeal alone." He touched her face. "I don't either."

"Why?" Maggie asked coldly. "Feeling sorry for me?"

"No. I feel responsible in a way."

"Responsible?"

"I've got things to tell you. Believe me, I wish I didn't have to, but it's time to stop lying." Mick reached deep inside himself for courage and said, "I was hired to look after you, Maggie."

"What?"

"Your uncle paid me to go to the island and watch over you. I sailed—"

"You were *paid*?" Maggie wrenched out of his arms and stumbled backward, staring.

"It's true. He hired me over a week ago when you left for the villa. He—"

"Oh, that makes it even better!" she interrupted harshly. She tottered away and caught her balance on the window frame. "Why didn't I see that possibility from the start?"

Mick joined her at the window. "I know it's not what you want to hear, but—"

She laughed once, unsteadily, and faced him by the window. "Of course I want to hear it. All of it! I suppose J.B. shelled out good money to see that I was taken to bed, too! Was that part of the deal?"

"Maggie—"

"*Was* it?" she demanded, trembling. "Did you tell him you left a satisfied customer? Did you get a bonus for that performance?"

"There was no performance," Mick snapped. "What happened between us was purely accidental."

"Accidental," Maggie repeated, taut as wire. "I see."

"No you don't see. That's not what I meant, and you know it."

"I don't know anything!" she exploded, wildly angry all of a sudden. "I only understand that people are always meddling in my life! And it wouldn't surprise me if you and J.B. felt it necessary to conspire so that my meager allotment of female hormones don't dry up forever!"

"Stop it," Mick ordered. He moved closer to take her into his arms, but Maggie pushed him violently away.

"Leave me alone. Get out of my house! Take your—your obnoxious little boy and go back to wherever you came from! Your job is finished now."

Mick stopped and dropped his hands to his sides, slowly curling them into fists. "You're right, my job is finished. That's not why I'm here."

"Why then?"

"I want to know what's happened. Why did you come dragging home a sack full of cash?"

"It's none of your—"

"Indulge me!" he shouted, losing control. Maggie flinched, but he plunged ahead, letting all his frustration pour out like hot lava. "I probably saved your kid's life after I dragged you out of the ocean when you were drowning, so you owe me a little something. Tell me what's going on! Are you paying off Bratton? Talk to me, damn you!"

"Yes," she said, breathless.

"That's all? He'll leave Elizabeth alone?"

"Yes."

"And the pictures? The photographs? You're buying those, too?"

She hesitated. "In time, yes."

"In time? What the hell does that mean?"

"I'm paying in installments. At the end, I'll get the photographs."

Rapid-fire, he asked more questions. "How many installments?"

"A—a few."

"How many, Maggie?"

She turned her head away, ashamed and sick with anxiety. "Four."

"How much money each time?"

"A lot," she said softly. "More than I have."

"There must be close to a hundred grand in that bag."

She nodded. "Yes."

Inside, Mick felt his anger deflate, leaving a horrid emptiness in its place. He realized he was gripping her tightly, and guilt rose up. He didn't remember the moment he'd grabbed her, but Maggie looked defeated and frightened. He'd been half the cause, this time. He loosened his grip, wishing he could comfort her and knowing she wouldn't let him.

He let his hands fall. More quietly, he asked, "When are you supposed to pay him?"

"Tonight." She used her shaky hands to rub the circulation back into her arms. "Seven o'clock. In the park."

"The park? The idiot's seen too many movies." Mick shook his head in derision. Then the glimmer of an idea asserted itself. "On the other hand, it might give us a chance."

"A chance?" Maggie lifted her face, and saw his expression. "No, Mick," she said at once. "Wait."

He began to pace. "It'll be dark by seven, and with luck the park will be—"

"*No*, I said!" Maggie blocked him, firmly. "Mick, listen to me. I want to go through with this. Ben has promised to leave us alone, and I believe him."

"You *believe* him? For heaven's sake—"

"I'm going to pay."

"Maggie, it's absolutely the wrong thing to do! You're going to get *nothing* and he'll have everything he wants. You can't—"

"Please! It's my choice! Have enough respect for me, at least, to let me make it."

Tears suddenly magnified her eyes, quivering on the edge of her eyelids and sending a pang shooting through Mick as he looked down into her sweet, upturned face. Her hands clutched his shirt, sending a throb of tension down through his body. Her beauty, her softness, tugged at his senses. But like a candle's glow, there was something more inside her, a warmth, an honesty, a mother's generosity, a lover's sweetness. Respect? He'd never known a woman he could respect more. Not even the one he'd married had been so inherently good as Maggie. Mick found himself reaching for her, grasping her, drawing her nearer.

Maggie resisted, watching his face and awaiting an answer.

Mick stared past her out the window for a moment, torn between doing what he knew was right and what Maggie wanted most. Slowly, he laced his fingers in her dark, silky hair. "All right," he said at last. "Pay him, if you think it's best. But I want one condition."

"No."

"Yes. Let me come along."

"Mick—"

"I don't need to talk to him. I won't even show myself, if you prefer. I just want to be there. You can hate me for it, but I want to be sure you aren't hurt."

Maggie's hands tightened on his chest for a second. Then, her voice muffled and ragged, she said. "I don't hate you."

Mick inhaled deeply, steadying himself against the rush of relief. "That helps," he murmured.

"Does it?" She tilted her face up once again, and her beautiful gray eyes reflected mistrust. How quickly she had changed her mind about him.

He bent slowly, unable to prevent himself from kissing her, in the back of his mind wanting to make her understand. She didn't resist, though he felt her tremor of indecision. Maggie's lips trembled, then melted under his. With a gentle, easy motion, he parted her mouth and tasted the moist sweetness of her with his tongue. She made a quiet sound—not a protest, but something else. Her hands slipped lower, then Mick felt them on his back, tentative, perhaps, but holding him close nevertheless. She gave in to the kiss, pouring all her pent-up emotion into the moment, giving everything, trusting him, seeking answers.

Mick held her tightly, wishing he could keep the kiss tender, but quickly realizing that one taste of Maggie was not enough. She had awakened his soul again, made him feel emotion again, healed the wound of his grief. He wanted to give something back, to reward and caress and adore her, but his body responded to her with lust. Perhaps she could feel how quickly she had aroused him.

Realizing himself, Mick drew back, afraid that one moment more would drive him over the edge of propriety.

Maggie's infernal, inconvenient, damnable propriety. He couldn't quite release her, though, and stood holding her loosely in his arms. Their foreheads bumped gently. Maggie wouldn't look at him. Her cheeks were pink. She would not speak. Maggie was not the kind of woman who would say what was on her mind. So it was up to him to make things right.

"Maggie," Mick began, absurdly uncertain, "a lot has happened. Most of it we couldn't help, but some of this mess we created ourselves. That morning at the villa—"

She stiffened. "We don't have to talk about that."

"I think we do. You hold back and cope, somehow, but I'm different. I had to keep a lot of secrets for a long time—from myself at first, then from you, and now—"

"Mick—"

"The morning we made love, I left because I—everything we did together reminded me of my wife. Of Victoria."

Maggie listened, then. Tense, perhaps, but quiet.

"I loved her very much," Mick said, steeling himself to tell Maggie everything. "But we had some problems at the end. She—Victoria started seeing someone else, and I—I didn't handle it with an open mind. After she died—"

Maggie gasped softly. "She's—"

"Yes, she's dead." He saw more tears start in Maggie's eyes, and he cradled her gently. "It's been a long time," he assured her softly. "I can't pretend I've been a saint since then, either. I started seeing other women pretty quickly, and I went to bed with a few of them. But with you, I—God, I can't explain. I just felt weird afterward. Guilty and—"

"Guilty?"

He shook his head, trying to organize his thoughts, pin down his emotions. "It's hard to understand," he said at last. "For the first time, I felt as if I'd betrayed her. It never happened before. I had to get away from you. It must have seemed—you must have felt—"

"I thought you didn't like it," she supplied.

He stared. "Didn't like it? Maggie—"

"It's all right," she said, hastily. "I'm not very good. It's hard for me to—"

"Good God, woman," Mick said roughly. "You're beautiful. You're warm and sexier than you seem to have any conception of. There's no reason in the world for you to feel inadequate. That's why I have to be honest with you."

"Honest?"

"About myself. Maggie, I—" Mick faltered. Carefully, he disengaged her hands and clasped them between his palms. He forced himself to look her straight in the eye. "You deserve a lover. You deserve a husband who can give you everything. Making love with you was incredible, and you make me happy when I'm with you. I'd like nothing better than to stay with you for a very long time."

She listened to him without blinking, without saying a word.

"But," Mick went on, doggedly, "you deserve a man who can love you the way you're capable of loving him. I'm a cripple when it comes to that, so after tonight I'll clear out of your life. Just understand that it's my fault, not yours."

Eight

Maggie longed to hold him, to make Mick feel better, to mother him, perhaps. But he broke away from her, spent from everything he'd blurted out. Maggie watched him pace and wished she could find the words to heal him. But he had learned the truth about relationships the hard way. When he opened his heart to love someone he had left himself vulnerable to pain. And the possibility of tragedy.

Abruptly, he needed action. "Let's get the show on the road," he said, swinging around. "When are you supposed to meet Bratton?"

Maggie called Cilla to come back and baby-sit again, and her cousin arrived within an hour.

"We're not going to tell her anything," Maggie ordered Mick while Cilla was hanging up her coat. "You understand? She's not to know about Ben. I told her we—that you and I were going on a date, so stick to the story."

"Sure thing," said Mick. But when Cilla joined them in the kitchen, he said, "Miss Cilla, you sure look like the kind of woman who's physically fit."

She eyed him warily. "Is this a pass, Mozzarella?"

"Sorry, no. I was just noticing. You go to exercise class? Or maybe you take self-defense?"

"Karate. So watch it."

"You bet," said Mick. "Your hands are probably registered weapons. But just in case you get attacked by Chuck Norris, do you carry any of that self-defense spray in your purse? Or one of those little alarm horns that can split an eardrum?"

Her expression of amazement deepened. "Yeah, I carry spray. You think I'm going to need it in the next minute or two?"

"No, I thought maybe you'd lend it to Maggie for tonight."

Cilla's eyes widened. "Just what kind of guy are you? I've heard of men with uncontrollable urges, but you—"

"Just lend it, will you?" Mick interrupted, quelling her with a wry look. "We're going to a pretty tough restaurant, and I don't want to have to punch the waitress if she gets aggressive."

Cilla dug out the spray can and handed it over, shaking her head. "I don't know, Maggie. This character is definitely unusual."

Maggie kissed her cousin. "Thanks, Cilla. You're a doll. I'm not sure when we'll be back. You can sleep in the guest room, if you like. Spider can stay with Elizabeth."

"I think I will bed down here," Cilla said. "It's a shorter walk to the office. And I'll also be here later if Mozzarella tries any funny business."

Ben Bratton's directions for the payoff had been so specific that Maggie had had to jot them down. She took the slip of paper with her.

Mick drove Maggie's station wagon to the park entrance Ben had designated but passed it and slid into a no-parking space along the curb farther down the block. He shut off the lights and the engine.

"This isn't where I'm supposed to meet Ben," Maggie said.

"I know. Listen up. I'll walk part of the way back with you, then fade into the bushes or mix with the crowd, all right? I'll be out of sight, but close enough if you need me. You hand over the dough, keep the conversation to a minimum and get back to the car by yourself. Here are the keys. Drive around the block and pick me up when Bratton is gone."

Maggie nodded, fumbled the keys and struggled to shove them into her coat pocket.

"Scared?" Mick asked, voice husky in the confines of the car.

"Petrified." And it was true. Though she had first wanted to hand over the money solo, Maggie felt ridiculously relieved to have Mick along. His expertise in such matters was some comfort. Still, she wished Ben hadn't planned such an elaborate melodrama. Her nerves were stretched tight.

Mick looped his hand around the nape of her neck and drew Maggie across the seat to kiss her lightly. He undoubtedly meant it to be casual, to bolster her courage, but Maggie accepted the kiss and her brain went blank. Inside, she was churned up all over again. Suddenly she wanted to hide in his arms, to sit in the darkness and spoon like lovers. But she imagined Mick would be businesslike and push her away.

"Don't be petrified," he said, unaware of the havoc he aroused in her. "It's a simple business transaction. What can go wrong?"

"Plenty of things!"

Mick shook his head. "Just remember that Bratton wants his money. Nothing's more important to him than that. If he gets mad and sends the pictures to a newspaper, he's killing the golden goose. If something goes wrong tonight, he'll just set up another meeting."

Mick tapped her chin, and Maggie saw the flash of his grin. "Hang tough, Miss Margaret," he said.

He was *pleased*, damn him! Happy to have a dangerous job to complete. He got out of the car, closed the door, and went around the hood almost jauntily to help Maggie out. He assisted her onto the sidewalk, glancing up and down the street to get his bearings. Scattered traffic moved along the rain-wet street, and a bus roared past, spewing exhaust. Perhaps three or four dozen tourists milled around the park entrance, including a gaggle of Japanese gentlemen sporting cameras and friendly smiles and a few teenagers clutching boom boxes.

With a single, sweeping glance, Mick took in the scene and registered the details. Satisfied, he turned up the collar of his jacket against the light drizzle that slanted through the air.

"Let's party," he said.

"Do you have to act so happy to be here?"

"Sorry," he replied, looking far from contrite. His grin was wickedly pleased.

Maggie tried to shoulder the canvas bag that contained one hundred thousand dollars. Somehow it now seemed heavier than it had earlier in the day, and she struggled to tug the strap over her shoulder. Mick helped, then took her arm and they walked toward the three brick archways of the park gate which loomed under a streetlamp that flickered off and on, casting neonlike flashes down the sidewalk and up into the leafless branches of the park trees.

Maggie clung to Mick's arms and tried to think brave thoughts. Their footsteps echoed eerily in the night air. Despite Mick's nearness, Maggie shivered. Icy raindrops struck her face, and the wind snatched at the hem of her coat. For a second, she wished she had given in when Mick suggested she exchange her skirt and sweater for jeans and boots.

At the gate, they hesitated, arm in arm. A tourist in a yellow rain slicker brushed past. Maggie looked up at Mick, wondering what came next, but she couldn't quite make out Mick's expression.

"Don't worry," he said, "It'll be fine."

It was the same tone he had used with her when they were making love.

Not seeing how shaken she was, he asked, "Have the spray in your pocket?"

"Yes, here."

"Good. Keep your hand on it. If Bratton gets fresh, use it. I'll buy Cilla another."

Maggie tried to smile, knowing he was making a joke to bolster her nerves. She said, "That won't be necessary."

Mick leaned towards Maggie and kissed her forehead. "Good luck."

Then he melted into the half darkness and the crowd, leaving Maggie alone in that bustling square.

She walked on, glancing nervously around. There was no reason to be afraid, but Maggie began to see danger lurking behind every tree. Could passersby detect the concern with which she clutched her bag? Perhaps one of the surly teenagers lounging against the brick wall had guessed she was carrying a fortune.

She pulled the sack closer against herself and set off down the sidewalk in search of the rendezvous spot. Anxiously, she tried to keep an eye on everyone who came close. One of the Japanese gentlemen brushed her arm, and Maggie spun around, instantly terrified.

The gentleman bowed. "Sorry, miss."

Without responding, Maggie hurried on. Twice, she glanced over her shoulder, certain she was being followed. As the darkness of the park enfolded her, she groped in her coat pocket until she found the cylinder of spray. She grasped it like a lifeline. In her chest, Maggie's heart beat crazily against her ribs. She could hardly breathe.

"Hey!"

A heavy hand landed on her shoulder.

Maggie cried out, and in the same instant brought the spray can out of her pocket and blasted her attacker square in the face.

"God almighty," Ben rasped. "What the hell?"

"Ben! Oh, heavens, I'm so sorry!"

"What—who do you think you are?"

"I was afraid," Maggie blurted out. "Why did you have to pick such a—a spooky place for this stupid meeting? Oh, Ben! How badly are you hurt?"

He choked and coughed. Tears streamed from his eyes. He tried spitting, but that didn't help. He even tore open his tie and the collar of his shirt. "Bad enough," he snapped. "What *is* that stuff? What's *wrong* with you?"

"I'm sorry!" Maggie cried. At the same time, she began to giggle helplessly. "I thought you were somebody else!"

"The Boston Strangler? Hell, I can't *see!*" He struggled to get a handkerchief from his trouser pocket and then tried to mop his streaming eyes.

"It was a mistake, Ben. Really, I'm sorry. Let me help. Here—"

He tore loose from her hands. "Let go of me! Hand over the money. I'm getting out of here!"

Maggie began to apologize again, but Ben yanked the shoulder bag so roughly from her that Maggie lost her balance and nearly fell.

"I'll be in touch," Ben snapped, and with that he stormed away. "This is one mistake you're going to regret!"

Maggie stared after him, blind to the rain and deaf to the sound of tourists milling around her. She watched Ben stalk off into the crowd, and inside she felt sick. What stupid mistake had her silly fears caused now?

At last she remembered what Mick had told her to do. Uncertainly, she set off for the car. She had difficulty inserting the ignition key, and when she pulled into traffic an oncoming bus blasted its horn at her. Maggie was still shaking badly when she rounded the block and Mick appeared in her headlights.

He came around to the driver's door and popped it open. "Slide across," he said. "I'll drive."

"I can do it," she insisted.

"You were all over the road just now," Mick admonished. "You'll give lady drivers a bad name. Slide over."

She obeyed and was absurdly glad when Mick took charge. Trembling, she covered her face with her hands. "I messed up," she said through her fingers.

Behind the wheel, Mick chuckled. "I saw. Nice move."

"You were watching?"

"From a discreet distance, don't worry. What happened?"

"I was scared! Walking around in the dark like that—and he came up so quickly I thought—it's just that—"

"Take it easy," Mick said kindly. "There's no need to cry now. It's over."

Startled, Maggie realized that she was on the brink of tears. She ordered herself to calm down and almost succeeded. After a few deep breaths she told Mick everything.

"I was scared," she admitted at last.

"He was counting on that, I'm sure. The jerk. He probably got the whole idea from a Movie of the Week."

Weakly, Maggie said, "He's really very smart, believe me."

"He's an amateur," Mick retorted, full of scorn.

Maggie realized she was shivering. Feebly, she pulled her coat closer around herself. "He—he threatened me when he left."

Mick glanced across at her. "The crack about regretting your mistake. Another line out of a tired script. When he cools down, he'll be happy with the dough."

"But that spray really hurt him. His eyes—"

Mick shrugged. "So he'll be uncomfortable for a few hours."

"That's enough time to get very angry. What if he—"

Mick interrupted harshly. "Will you stop worrying? You're the only woman I know who'd feel sorry for a creep like that at a time like this!"

"I can't help it! It's my life at stake, mine and Elizabeth's! He threatened me," she insisted, voice cracking. "You can be perfectly calm because it's not your child in the balance! I'm allowed to worry! I'm allowed to worry myself to a frazzle if I choose!"

"Steady," Mick warned.

"I don't have to be steady anymore," she exploded. "If I want a good cry, dammit, I'll have one!"

At that declaration, Mick started to laugh.

Maggie boiled over. "You think I'm ridiculous, don't you? This is all a game to you! You don't give a damn about any of it!"

She had managed to hang on to her control until then. But Mick's momentary hesitation, his split-second failure to answer her question brought the point home clearly. He didn't care a whit for her. She was alone and in trouble and there was nobody who could get her out of the mess but herself. And she had nearly bungled it.

Maggie hid her face in her hands. Choking, she held down three gargantuan sobs. The fourth she couldn't keep secret. In the next instant, Maggie was crying hard.

Mick pulled over and stopped the car.

Then he slid across the seat and took Maggie in his arms, saying nothing. She fought him at first, weakly punching at his chest, but Mick subdued her effortlessly.

"Maggie," he said, his voice barely a murmur in her ear.

"I'm not crying," she snapped, then hiccoughed violently.

He petted her hair, holding her close as moonlight spilled across them through the windshield. "All right, you're not," he agreed. "But if you were, it would be understandable. My sweet, gallant, brave Miss Margaret. You did just fine. It's okay to let off a little steam."

"I—I hate being weak. I feel like a prize fool!"

"You're not weak, and you've never been a fool. You're ten times tougher than you think you are. You were brave tonight, and that's astonishing considering what you've been through. Relax now." He stroked her chin with one gentle finger and pressed a soft kiss against her throat. "Relax," he coaxed.

Mick felt the tension ease in Maggie's body. He cuddled her in the cool light of the moon, warming her until she ceased to tremble and congratulating himself for keeping cool in the face of her pain. Gradually, though, he sensed that Maggie's tension hadn't just evaporated. It had simply begun to soak into him instead. As he sat with her, holding Maggie gently, Mick recognized the signs. He was holding his breath, willing his body not to respond to her. He forced his eyes shut to avoid looking down at the silvery gleam of tears on her lovely face. He'd promised! No more lovemaking. It would be disastrous.

She moved her head and laid her cheek against his chest, perhaps an innocent change of position as far as she was concerned, but a distinctly electric one for Mick. He ground his teeth at the sensation that rose within him. Her hair smelled sweetly feminine, and a wisp of it tickled his nose. Mick drew a shuddering breath of air. He had just enough

self-control left to avoid pressing her down against the up-
holstery and unbuttoning her clothes.

"I'm all right, now," she said at last. But she made no
effort to get out of his embrace.

"You're sure?"

With her cheek snugly against his shirt, she nodded. Her
right hand lay on Mick's chest, and she smoothed it down-
ward, instinctively seeking his heartbeat.

Mick's breath caught. He trapped her hand in his and
gently pried it away. Already his blood had begun to stir.
The least he could do was keep that secret from her. He sat
back. "Ready to go home now?"

She looked him straight in the eye. Hers still shone with
the vestige of tears, but she could hear how false his voice
sounded. "I'm sorry," she whispered. "I'm not making this
any easier on you, am I?"

"Maggie," he began, but his voice rasped and he couldn't
finish.

She tried to smile, but the result was a trembling attempt
that shot a dart of sadness through Mick's heart.

He turned away from her swiftly and jammed the car into
gear. Not speaking, he pulled out onto the street again. He
didn't glance at Maggie, but sensed that she had to put her
face to the window. He hadn't a clue what she was thinking. Perhaps pity was foremost in her mind. Maybe frustration. Perhaps she cried again, but it wasn't fear that
gripped her anymore. Mick tightened his hands on the
steering wheel until his palms hurt.

They arrived back at her house without speaking. Maggie got out of the car and led the way to her backdoor, which
she unlocked herself. She preceded him inside. Reluctantly,
Mick followed.

The kitchen was quiet. Cilla had apparently gone to bed.
A light over the stove was burning softly, casting a glow

across the cheery room. Maggie didn't turn on any more lights, and Mick was grateful.

"I'm sorry," she said at last, draping her coat over the back of one of the chairs. "For making you uncomfortable back there."

"It wasn't your fault," he said, keeping a safe distance. "I can't seem to help the way you make me feel. You're a beautiful woman, Miss Margaret."

She faced him then. And time stretched. Between them lay six feet of empty space, a distance that could be crossed in a blink. Maggie stood very still. Her eyes were wide and steady. Mick thought he could see her pulse beating in the soft flesh of her throat.

"Stay with me," Maggie whispered at last. "Just for tonight."

Mick strode to her almost before the words were out of her mouth. He seized her in his hands, bending her body until she fit against the lean length of his own. "I want to," he said tightly, holding her. "Believe me, I do. But I can't, Maggie. It's not fair to you."

She wound her slim arms around his neck, tipping her face up to his. "I'm not asking you to marry me."

He grinned a little, tracing the line of her cheekbone with his finger. "I know that. And if you were anyone else, I'd have carried you up those stairs already. But—"

Maggie curled her hands in his shirt. "Do it," she said softly. "Please."

"You need more than I can give, Maggie!"

"It's enough," she said simply. "I'm in love with you, Mick."

He stared deeply into her eyes.

She smiled back, and something close to joy dawned in her face. "It's true. Whether you return the same feeling or not doesn't matter. Let me love you."

Mick kissed the edge of her mouth. He fought the urge to plunder her lips, giving her a gentle kiss instead. "Maggie, we have to talk about this. I've done things you're going to—"

"Never mind our differences."

"It's more than that. I've got to explain before you do something you'll—"

"I can't help the way I feel," she intervened. "It's the kind of person I am."

"You're talking about lust. A biological impulse that—"

"I'm allowed to have urges, too," she said. "You told me so yourself. And if you really want me also, what's the harm?"

Mick closed his eyes. "I don't want to hurt you, Maggie."

"You can only hurt me by saying no. I need you tonight, Mick. You've lent me your strength before. I—I need it again."

He didn't respond. He couldn't. Inside, he was seething. Passion grew within him like a fantastic beast. He didn't want to think about what he'd done to her, the things he needed to explain, how he'd been just as manipulating as every other man in her life. But suddenly Mick wanted only to lose himself in her—just for a little while.

She peeled off his tweed jacket, wanting to strip him down until she could run her fingers over every inch of his golden skin. On tiptoes, she kissed his mouth, his cheek, his throat. In a moment, she would lead him upstairs. At her bedside, she would undress him slowly. Mick let the erotic images unfold in his mind.

With her nose, she teased his earlobe. "What can I do," she coaxed, "to convince you?"

Mick gave a shuddering laugh. "Amazing woman."

"Only with you," Maggie murmured. She tossed his jacket across one of the kitchen chairs. It missed and slipped to the floor, giving a quiet *thunk* as it landed on the tile. The sound brought Mick abruptly back to reality.

"What's that?" Maggie demanded.

She bent to retrieve the jacket and the compact, rectangular packet that had fallen from one of his pockets. "Mick, it's money!"

"Yes," he said. One minute earlier his veins had thundered with desire. Now he felt his insides shrivel with misgivings. "This is what I had to explain about."

Maggie snatched up the packet of bills and stared. "This is *my* money! The cash I paid Ben—it's—Mick, what's the meaning of this?"

Mick took her by the arms very firmly and led her to the counter. He leaned there and held Maggie fast. "Darling, if Ben pulls something nasty in the next day or two, it won't be because you sprayed him with a little Mace."

"What are you talking about?"

Every vestige of warmth disappeared, leaving Mick cold and determined. "I switched the money." Coming clean, he said, "I'm as bad as your uncle J.B., I know, but you wouldn't listen, and I didn't know what else to do. Before we left, I stuffed the bag with a couple of magazines and left just one set of bills on top, in case you peeked. Ben didn't get a hundred grand. He's got about twenty-five hundred dollars and a couple of back issues of *The New Yorker* along with a note from me that should start him thinking about renegotiating the deal."

"You—! You had no right!"

She struggled to yank free, but Mick hung on grimly. "I knew I'd never get you to agree to a plan today, so I bought us a little time. Ben—"

"How could you do such a thing?" Maggie cried. "You risked my daughter—"

"Elizabeth wasn't in danger. Ben doesn't want custody, you said it yourself. He—"

"You don't know him," Maggie snapped. "When he loses his temper he can be completely irrational. This situation might push him over the edge! I can't believe you'd do something like—you really don't give a damn about me, do you?"

"Of *course* I care for you! Maggie, I'd never have made love with you the first time if I didn't have some—"

"Oh, spare me!" Maggie cried. She shoved out the swinging door and hurried through the dining room.

Mick followed. "Maggie, stop."

"I should have thrown you out this morning!" she cried. Enraged, she stormed into the half-dark living room. And she nearly tripped over something in the middle of the floor.

Behind her, Mick flicked on the lamp and swore ferociously.

The next few seconds passed in a kaleidoscope of horror. Cilla lay on the living room rug, her arms bound behind her back, her legs wrapped with a telephone cord and a pair of panty hose tied tightly around her head in a gag. Her eyes were wide open and furious. Around her, the living room was a wreck. She hadn't gone down without a fight.

Maggie choked back a scream and fell to her knees. Frantically, she tore at the gag in Cilla's mouth. Her fingers were shaking too badly to untie the knot.

Mick shouldered her aside. In seconds he freed Cilla from the gag and set to work on her legs.

Her mouth free, Cilla began to swear a blue streak.

"What happened?" Mick demanded, his voice cracking like a whip. "Cut the dramatics and tell us."

"A guy broke in here," Cilla said rapidly. "Rang the bell and forced his way in. We struggled, and damn you, Mozzarella, don't make a single crack about Chuck Norris! He hit me on the head with a damn lamp and tied me up. God, what a headache! Get your hands off my knees, dammit!"

"The kids," Mick said, looking straight into Maggie's eyes.

Maggie was already on her feet. She ran for the stairs and flew up to the bedrooms, her heart pounding so hard in her throat that she nearly choked.

She flung open Elizabeth's door and rocked to a stop. Light from the hall splashed across the bed and fell magically across Elizabeth's face where the child lay burrowed in her covers. For the first time in a full minute, Maggie drew a ragged breath. It came out like a sob. She pushed the door wider.

Then her heart ceased to beat entirely. The other side of Elizabeth's ruffled bed was empty. The lacy blankets were thrown back. The pillow was missing, too.

Mick thrust into the room, pushing Maggie aside. He turned on the light.

Maggie said, "Ben took Spider instead. My God, Mick, he's taken Spider."

Nine

Maggie ran down the stairs, brushing past Cilla, who was on her way up. Cilla caught her arm. "Maggie—"

She didn't stop. She went directly to the kitchen and began to rip through the pockets of Mick's jacket until she had collected every packet of money. She shoved them into a paper bag, snatched her car keys from the countertop and let herself out the back door without a backward look.

No more games. She intended to drive to Baltimore and hand over the money immediately. The only thing worse than losing Elizabeth, Maggie thought, would be having Mick lose his son.

She started her car with a roar and pulled out onto the street.

On top of the excruciating pain in his eyes, Ben Bratton nearly suffered a heart attack. He carried the sleeping child up to his condominium and tucked her in bed, then showered, put on his pajamas and was making himself a cup of herbal tea when he looked up and saw an apparition in striped blue pajamas wander into his kitchen. The kid rubbed his eyes and then looked at Ben like a grumpy gnome.

Ben stared back. "Who the hell are you?"

The kid said, "Who the hell are *you*?"

Ben dropped his cup and splashed herbal tea all over the butcher block counter. He made a quick calculation and realized he'd made a very, very large blunder.

"Listen, kid," he said carefully, "there's been a mistake."

The little boy's dark eyes filled with rage. His face tightened. His fists stiffened at his sides. Suddenly he was transformed before Ben's eyes from a sleepy Puck into a belligerent holy terror.

His voice filled the room. *"Where's my dad?"*

"Uh—" Ben thought fast. The last thing he needed was a hysterical kid on his hands. Snatching Elizabeth hadn't seemed like a bad idea. Maggie wasn't about to go to the police for help. But stealing a kid he'd never clapped eyes on before suddenly looked like a very serious criminal act.

Ben knelt down and manufactured a friendly smile. "Your dad is—well, he's—I'm sure he'll be in touch very soon. Listen, little boy, how about if I make you a nice snack and we—"

The kid interrupted, "I want pancakes."

"Pan—? Well, I don't think I have any syrup. How about some nice bran cereal and—"

"Doughnuts," the kid said firmly. "It's almost Saturday, right? My dad always lets me have doughnuts on Saturdays."

From the cunning expression on the little monster's face, Ben figured he was lying. Still, anything to keep him happy until Ben decided what to do next seemed like a wise move.

"Okay, doughnuts," Ben proclaimed, heading for the phone book with alacrity. "I wonder if doughnut shops deliver?"

The kid followed Ben into the living room, looking around with interest when Ben snapped on the lights. "You got any toys?" he asked.

"Uh, no, but—"

"Hey, neat! A piano!" He bolted for the instrument, and before Ben could protest he was banging on the keys with all his strength.

Ben clamped his teeth shut to keep from yelling. Better keep the kid happy. With the piano booming in the background, Ben dialed the doughnut shop and shouted into the receiver until he convinced the store manager to deliver. "I *know* it's after midnight! I thought you people made doughnuts round the clock! Yes, yes, all right. I promise to buy six dozen doughnuts!—but only if you get them here fast!"

He hung up the phone and turned around in time to see the little boy leap off the piano bench onto the pastel sofa. The brat started jumping up and down.

"Hey, this is neat!"

"Don't—" Ben's command ended in a strangled yelp. Like some kind of demented acrobat, the kid jumped from one sofa to the other and back again, landing just inches from a Chinese lamp. "Wait!" Ben cried. "Stop!"

The kid stopped, but looked far from happy. Ben doubled his effort to look friendly. "Say," he wheedled, "how about telling me your name?"

The kid's suspicious look deepened. He folded his arms across his chest. "I'm not supposed to talk to strangers."

Ben laughed heartily. At least, he hoped it sounded hearty. "Strangers? I'm not a stranger! I'm your Uncle Ben. Hasn't dear old dad mentioned me before?"

"No." Sullen and suspicious, the kid went on glaring.

"Well, your dad and I go back a long way. Honest, we do. A long, long way! Now, what's your name?"

The kid looked tough a little longer, then relented. "Spider."

"What?"

The kid glowered. "Spider. How come you know my dad, but you don't know me?"

"Uh, well, I *do* know you, Spider, but I—I just forgot, that's all. I just—listen, I have to make a phone call. Until the doughnuts come, why don't you—"

"I want to play a game."

"A game?"

"Yeah. My dad and me always play pretend games on the weekends. I want to play Cowboys and Indians."

"Well, that sounds reasonable." Ben began to edge away. "I'll just make a quick telephone call and then I'll join you."

"Great. You got any rope?"

"Rope?"

Cilla picked up Maggie's telephone on the first ring. "Yes?"

"Listen," said a desperate male voice. "I think we ought to negotiate."

"Mozzarella? Is that you?"

"Who's this?"

Cilla realized her caller was not Maggie's friend Mick. She strained her ears to listen to the background noise on the other end of the line. Unless her imagination was playing tricks, she thought she could hear Indian war whoops. "Hey," she said, "is this the son of a bitch who hit me over the head with a lamp?"

The voice groaned. "Oh, God, it's you! Where's Maggie?"

"How should I know? Nobody tells me anything! She went charging out of here like a bat out of hell and a man I'm really starting to get the hang of just stole my car and went after her. Now tell me—"

"Never mind," said the voice. "I'm in big trouble! No, no!" he yelled. "Wait! Not in my food processor!"

The line went dead.

Maggie charged up the two flights of stairs that lead to Ben's condo, the paper bag flapping in her arms. She pounded on his door.

A full three minutes later, after Maggie had nearly beaten dents in the door, Ben opened it a crack and peeked out. He looked wild-eyed, but the relief in his face was obvious when he spotted Maggie.

"Honey!" he cried joyfully. "Am I glad to see you!"

Maggie's jaw dropped at his welcome as she stepped into his foyer and closed the door behind herself. Ben's appearance startled her, for he was dressed in torn pajamas with a leather belt slung down around his hips in the fashion of a gunslinger, his hair askew, and there was a length of string wrapped around his neck like a miniature noose. On his forehead, a bruise had begun to show.

"Thank God you're here," he declared. "This kid gives me the creeps! He's a *maniac*! He's dangerous, I tell you! Please, you're going to take him back, aren't you?"

Like a football blocker, Maggie used her right hand to push Ben against the wall and out of her way. Her high-heeled shoes clicking, she entered the apartment and made a quick search. She found Spider at the kitchen table preparing to set fire to a heap of rolled newspapers with a kitchen match. He had the leaf of a houseplant stuck into his wiry hair, and judging by the food coloring he'd smeared on his face, he was thoroughly caught up in playing Indian.

"Spider!"

He blew out the match and whipped the evidence behind his back all in the same motion. The face he turned up to Maggie was cherubic. "Hi!" he said.

Maggie swooped him up in her arms and hugged Spider for all she was worth. So intense was her relief that she nearly choked on a sob. Spider laughed at the strangled sound she made. Maggie managed a grim sort of smile back at him.

Then, carrying the boy like a sack of groceries, she marched back through the apartment to Ben. She thrust the bag of money into his hands.

"There," she snapped. "There's your stupid money. If you try a trick like this again, Ben Bratton, I swear I'll call the police. To hell with my reputation and my uncle and my daughter's mental health! If you endanger the life of my child or anyone else's child again, I will see you slapped in jail!"

"Maggie, I—"

"Do you understand?"

Astonished by her rage, her tone of voice, her quaking, unsuppressed fury, Ben could only nod.

"Good," she growled. "Now get out of my way."

Ben stepped aside like a sleepwalker, and Maggie whipped open the door.

Mick was just clearing the top step in a powerful leap, and he came through the door like a springing tiger. Maggie was powerless to stop him.

Ben flung himself back, but it was too late. Mick seized him by the throat and jammed the lighter man back against the wall so hard his head thumped and left a web of cracks in the plaster. Ben's eyes seemed to spin in his head.

"Mick, stop!"

Enraged, Mick only tightened his hands around Ben's neck, forcing his whole body higher on the wall. Ben kicked frantically, making garbled gasps.

"Mick, don't! You'll kill him!"

Maggie tried to wedge herself between the men. Spider, still in her arms, cried out, and it was that sound that finally penetrated Mick's fog of rage. He checked himself. His face, still a frightening mask of absolute fury, showed no mercy whatsoever. But he loosened his grip on Ben's neck. Slowly, he let go until Ben slid down the wall and landed unsteadily on his own two feet.

Ben feebly put his hands to his injured throat. He coughed and stumbled as far from Mick's rage as he could get.

Mick swung around on Maggie, and before he could make another move, Maggie thrust his son into his arms. He hugged the boy against his chest, and looked directly over Spider's tousled head at Maggie.

"Thank you," he said, watching her face.

Maggie nodded. Shaken by what had nearly happened, she leaned weakly against the wall.

"I'm okay," Spider piped up. "Honest, Dad. I didn't do anything bad. I was a good guest."

Ben choked, his eyes still protruding.

"Let's go," Maggie said.

"Wait," croaked Ben. He plucked at Maggie's sleeve. "I think I get it now. You've got a boyfriend or something. That's who sent the note. I didn't find that until after I took the kid, honest. I couldn't figure out where—how this kid got into—"

"Shut up, Ben," Maggie said, not in the mood to hear another syllable.

Ben scuttled after them, trying frantically to block Maggie's departure. "Listen, I didn't mean any harm, really." He gave a convulsive swallow. "The kid nearly killed me, anyway! Please—"

"Just drop it," Maggie said.

He made a grab for her arm, but Mick was there to block him. Ben stared up at Mick, his hand straying nervously to his throat.

Maggie touched Mick's arm. "Let's go," she said quickly, before he started anything else. He turned without a word, and Maggie hurried after him.

Ben slammed the door behind them.

Maggie never flinched. She followed Mick as he started down the stairs with Spider in his arms. At that moment she thought she'd follow him to the ends of the earth.

At the bottom of the stairs, Mick turned. She could see the anger still boiling in his face.

"It's all right," she said at once. "It's over."

"Like hell it is."

"Mick, please—"

"You may be able to turn the other cheek, Maggie, but I can't. He's got something I want, and I'm going to get it back. All I have to do now is figure out how."

"Mick, please, it's over now. I'm sure he'll send the pictures and I'll—"

"Like hell he will. He's going to bleed you to death before he gives up anything. I'm going to stop him, Maggie, and nothing you can say will talk me out of it this time." He glared back up the stairs. "I'm getting into that place and tear it apart."

"You can't," Spider volunteered, stifling a yawn. "At least not tomorrow. He's having a party."

"A party?" Mick repeated. He looked straight at Maggie and this time his eyes gleamed with something other than anger.

"No," she began quickly. "Mick, you can't possibly—"

Pure pleasure dawned on his face. "Crash the party? Oh, darling love, you'd better believe I will."

Maggie seized his arm. "Mick! You can't! He'll throw you out! He'll call the police! He'll—"

"He won't do a damn thing," Mick interrupted. "Not if you're with me."

Maggie couldn't speak. Her mouth seemed no longer connected to her brain.

Mick grinned. "I'm going to nail the bastard," he said. "And you're going to help."

Ten

When they got back to Maggie's house at four in the morning, even Mick was too tired to make plans. They all needed sleep.

Maggie stripped off her clothes, barely managed to pull her nightgown over her head and was climbing between the covers when Mick let himself through the connecting door of the bathroom. He was yawning and unbuttoning his shirt.

"Cilla will be shocked," Maggie mumbled.

"Cilla is impervious to shock," Mick replied, sitting on the other side of the bed to pull off his shoes.

"G'night," said Maggie when he settled in beside her.

"G'night," Mick murmured. He pulled her body tight against his and went to sleep almost immediately, blowing a worn-out sigh along the nape of her neck.

Smiling, Maggie luxuriated in a cocoon of tired contentment for a time, reveling in the newfound closeness with this no-nonsense man of action. Their arms and legs tangled to-

gether as if they had shared a bed for years, and even in
sleep he murmured her name and folded her body against
his own. Surely, she thought, he loved her just a little. With
that feeling glowing in her mind, she let sleep overcome her.

Gradually Maggie returned to the land of the living, but
she woke slowly, enjoying the heat of Mick's splendid frame
against her own, the rhythm of his breathing and the
knowledge that he'd spent the night in her arms. Dozing, her
mind was bathed in a tide of lazily erotic images. When she
could stand it no longer, she woke completely and turned
toward him.

Mick was sitting up, pillows stuffed behind his back, a
sheaf of papers in his hand. Heaven knew how long he'd
been awake already, but he was hard at work. Maggie
watched him for a time, absorbing details. How the curling
hair on his chest swirled counterclockwise, how thick his
lashes were, how amazingly well-knit his whole body was.
Not aware of her observation, Mick chewed on the eraser of
a pencil. He wore a pair of horn-rimmed glasses that Maggie had never seen before, and it seemed that the glasses were
the only thing he was wearing. His chest and shoulders were
bare in the pale morning light, and the position of the sheet
strongly suggested a lack of other clothing as well.

"You know," Maggie mumbled at last, "I'd never have
let you sleep with me if I'd known you were farsighted."

Mick laughed. "Awake finally?"

"Partially conscious. What time is it? What are you
doing?" She struggled to sit up and rub her eyes at the same
time.

"It's about nine-thirty. Cilla's downstairs with the kids,
I think. And I'm making lists. Here. Draw me a sketch of
Bratton's apartment, will you? I just need to add a couple
of things to these notes and then we can get started."

Maggie tilted a rueful glance in his direction. "Has anyone ever complained before about your lack of romance?"

Chagrined, Mick peeked over the top of his papers at her. Maggie smiled sleepily back at him and wiggled her finger in a come-hither gesture. Mick took off his glasses, and his dark eyes filled with sparkle as they traveled from her face down to the slender curves of her body beneath the sheet.

"Forgive my bad manners," he said, stowing the glasses and papers in one swift movement. He gathered Maggie into his arms and rolled, pressing her down into the bed beneath him. His body rode deliciously over hers, taut and strong. Maggie's hair cascaded across the pillow, and Mick filled his hands with it, balancing his weight on his elbows. Maggie sighed with delight.

Mick looked onto the softness of her eyes and once again felt the warm rise of pleasure that had filled him when he woke and watched her sleep for a time. Her special inner radiance had shone even then. She had a kind of peace inside, he acknowledged, that drew him like a magnet, yet caused anything but peace in response.

"I love waking up with you," Maggie said huskily, lacing her fingers in his hair.

Her trusting smile brought an ache to his chest. "Maggie, I—"

"Nothing's changed," she said, her lips touching his to quell his protest with angelic softness. "Make love with me."

His heart thumped once and seemed to stop, suspended for a painful instant as he realized what she meant. She knew his limitations. And they didn't matter. She was willing to accept him without those all-important words, without a commitment. She loved him, and she didn't demand a declaration in return. Instinctively, Mick moved against her, perfecting the contact of their two bodies until her pliant breasts were firmly pressed against his chest.

He should have refused her. But whatever he felt for this woman—he wasn't able to give the emotion a name yet—

could not be denied. The hot, primitive yearning she kindled in him was too strong. Maggie was perfect. He found her mouth with his, and hers were not the only lips that trembled with barely suppressed emotion. She had just begun to plumb the depths of her own sensuality, and he was the man with whom she had chosen to share it. When they parted, Maggie whispered his name as if dedicating the sweetness of that first morning kiss. The sound was so hushed, so tender, that Mick thought he'd never heard his name spoken so poignantly before.

He laid his cheek against her breast and released a taut, pent-up breath. He had the power to hurt her, and he prayed for the strength to get up and leave her before he inflicted too painful a wound. But he was weak in spirit. Already longing had begun to burn too brightly inside him. He couldn't fight both his own desire and the sweet demand of Maggie's fingers as they feathered along his skin.

Unable to stop himself, Mick caressed his way down Maggie's slim curves and with a reverence tempered by passion, he freed her of the last garment between them. There were no sexual games after that, no teasing or coy provocations. He made love to her without preamble, sinking hungrily within Maggie's welcoming body, deeper and deeper into the sweet darkness of her yielding warmth, watching her eyes flicker with the intensity of pleasure, tasting her joyous mouth. She wrapped her arms around him and for a long, exquisite moment they lay locked together, breathing as one soul.

As if signaled by some inner magic neither of them understood, the fluid movement began. Moving in delicious unison, they climbed the sensual heights, moving more profoundly with each passing heartbeat until at last Mick lost control and thrust so hard and fiercely that Maggie cried out in release. She surrendered to the storm, pulsing around him, drawing Mick tighter and deeper until he became a part of her, joined in passion, clasped to her heart. He echoed her abandoned cry with his own deep growl as they burst over the edge of a shimmering horizon and soared together into a space so sweet, so perfect it could only be complete fulfillment.

As slowly as a tumbling autumn leaf, they drifted earthward after that, reluctantly reentering the world of reality.

They lay in silence, forehead to forehead, caressing languidly, breathing in synchronization, hearts beating as one. Mick had only to open his eyes now and then to absorb the warmth of Maggie's sated gaze and the unspoken declaration of love it contained.

Mick stroked the porcelain planes of her face, wondering how the beauty of one woman could move him so completely.

"I can't believe," he said softly, "that you don't hate me after what I did last night."

She smiled. "I was angry," she admitted. "But I can understand why you switched the money."

"I thought I could buy you some time, then convince you not to give in to Ben."

She touched his face. "I know. I wasn't ready then. I was afraid."

"And now?"

Her smile returned, looking braver. "I'm prepared to try."

Mick grinned. "I have a feeling you're going to be a formidable adversary, Miss Margaret."

She sighed and stretched catlike beneath him. "I'm not feeling formidable at the moment. Can't we just stay here all day? And take care of Ben later?"

"Your cousin is probably dying of curiosity. Besides, if we're going to pull this off, it's high time we got to work."

Maggie traced the line of his cheek, clearly as unwilling to abandon their shared intimacy as he was. "Exactly what have you got planned?"

"In a nutshell? To retrieve your money and get Bratton off your back forever."

Maggie's eyes filled with worry. "But he'll send the pictures to the newspaper office or—"

"Anything's possible," said Mick, silencing her with a swift kiss. "But he can't send them anywhere if we steal them first."

Maggie's hands tightened on his shoulders. "Mick!"

He cocked a questioning look down at her. "I got the feeling last night that you were ready to do anything. Are you still with me? I've got a plan."

Maggie hesitated as her old anxieties rose to the surface of her mind. Her fingers played nervously along the ridge of muscle in his arms. "Are you sure it will work?"

"Only if you succeed in the tough part."

"What's that?"

Mick broadened his most devious grin. "Dear Miss Margaret's got to teach me how to act at a black-tie party."

Maggie drew him down to kiss her deeply one last time. "Anything's possible."

There was no alternative to renting a suit of evening clothes for Mick, and Maggie took care of that expeditiously.

"No pink ruffled shirts," was Mick's only edict.

That evening, she helped him dress, but not before Mick had thoroughly reviewed his plan with her. Together they drew sketches, studied floor plans and evaluated their chances. Maggie alternated between respect for Mick's attention to detail and frustration that they couldn't just plunge ahead and get the job done. As she knotted his tie, he even insisted she repeat the steps aloud, coaching when she faltered.

"We've got to get this perfect," Mick said for the third time that day. "One little mistake could blow everything."

Meekly, Maggie bowed her head. "I'll do my best."

He lifted her chin and smiled encouragingly. "I know. There's just one more problem."

"What's that?"

He stepped back to appraise the velour bathrobe Maggie had donned after her shower. "Don't get me wrong," he said, nodding at the robe. "You look delectable in this thing. But haven't you got something a little—um—flashier?"

"Flashier?" Maggie pirouetted to examine herself in the full-length mirror on her closet door. "Dear sir, do I look like the kind of woman who owns one single thing that approaches flash?"

From behind, Mick wrapped his arms around her. Their eyes met in the mirror, dark and light, both full of laughter and a new intimacy. In his dinner jacket, Mick looked nothing short of marvelous. His fallen-angel good looks were heightened by the clean lines of the jacket and the elegant white shirt and perfect black tie. The sight of him took Maggie's breath away.

Surreptitiously, he began to loosen the belt on her robe, all the while holding her gaze in the mirror. "You'd look flashy in jeans," he said. "In anything. I remember exactly how you looked the moment we met. That white bathing suit?"

Smiling, Maggie closed her eyes. "Oh, dear, that was a mistake, wasn't it?"

"If you wanted to look like a spinster schoolteacher, yes. I thought it looked great." He slipped the robe open and smoothed his hands down her sides. "Your body is beautiful," he murmured in her ear, then nibbled on her lobe to punctuate the thought. In the mirror, her reflection trembled.

"Mick," she whispered, quivering as he cupped her breasts and caressed them. "We've got a party to attend."

He groaned softly while pressing kiss after kiss down the length of her throat. Maggie could feel the tight columns of his thighs behind her. She rested her palms against the warm muscle and dropped her head back against his chest. For a moment, she longed to forget about the night ahead. Her own bedroom had taken on a quiet yet compelling sensuality that she was loath to leave.

"We'll come back," Mick said. "Soon."

"With something to celebrate?"

"Yes. And, Miss Margaret, I know ways to celebrate that are going to make your head spin."

Maggie laughed and pushed him away, gathering the robe around herself once more. "Until then, let's keep our thoughts clean. Leave me alone now, will you? I'm going to get dressed."

"I'll help," Mick offered with a grin, tugging at her robe.

Firmly, she guided him to the bedroom door and opened it. "No, you'll just cause trouble. There's one important thing you've got to learn about me."

He paused in the doorway, bemused. "What's that?"

"I need a half hour of absolute peace to get dressed in. After that, you may have my complete attention."

"Complete?" Mick pressed. "That's a promise?"

"A promise. Now, run along. Go play with the children. Cilla should be here any minute, though. Can you two get along without a referee?"

"I'll try," Mick said. "But I won't speak for her."

True to her word, Maggie used exactly half an hour to make herself over. The dress she chose was a smashing white sequined number she'd worn to a Kennedy Center benefit performance. The sleeves were long and close-fitting, the

neckline plunged and for once she did not use a safety pin
to render it more modest and the hem touched the top of the
black velvet bows on her shoes. A slit to her knee had
seemed daring the first time Maggie wore the dress, but tonight she used a valuable five minutes to open it higher on
her thigh and baste the seams closed again. In her ears
Maggie wore her grandmother's diamond earrings, which
flashed in the lamplight, and she decided to leave her throat
bare. In recent days, she had come to accept her own soft
skin as adornment enough. She brushed her hair into a
loose, dark cloud, and secured it over one ear with a silver
clip.

With a black velvet wrap over her arm, she descended the
stairs.

Cilla had arrived and was setting up a Monopoly game on
the cocktail table with Elizabeth. Both of them looked up at
Maggie's entrance. Cilla looked startled. Elizabeth gasped.

"Mama! You look like a princess!"

Mick was stretched out on the sofa with Spider crawling
on his chest, but at Maggie's arrival, he sat up as if hypno-
tized and set Spider on his feet. He stood up, too, and came
to Maggie's side, his eyes glowing appreciatively.

He took her hand. "Like a princess," he agreed, and
kissed her there in front of everyone.

Cilla was looking wryly amused by the time he released
Maggie. "You two clean up pretty nicely," she admitted,
folding her arms across her chest. "A special evening
ahead?"

"Yes," said Maggie, smiling up at Mick.

"Hmm," said Cilla. "A jaunt to Monte Carlo, perhaps?
Or just a straight trip to Niagara Falls?"

"We'll let you know," said Mick, enfolding Maggie in her
velvet wrap. "Don't wait up, Cilla."

In the car, Maggie had to wrestle her way out of Mick's
arms.

"What's the matter with you?" she cried, laughingly holding him off. "I thought we were supposed to concentrate on Ben tonight."

"That was before you put on this dress. Come here. What's that thing made of, anyway? It feels like—"

"Mick!"

"All right, all right."

The drive back to Ben's Baltimore condo took an hour, but once on the road Mick gathered his thoughts and began to go over the plan once more, rehearsing the steps with Maggie. "What kind of guests should we expect?" he asked. "Will you know any of Bratton's friends?"

"Ben doesn't have any friends," Maggie said at last. "At least, none that I ever met. When we were seeing each other, he made friends with people I socialized with. He's a loner, essentially."

Mick snorted. "You sound sorry for the guy."

"I am, in a way. He's very charming, but he feels he has to use that charm all the time. I think he'd be a nice man if he'd just—if he'd accept himself."

Mick shook his head. "You're amazing."

"Because I can feel compassion for a pathetic man?"

"Because you can feel anything at all for the jerk who's making a mess out of your life."

Maggie sighed. "I can't hold a grudge. He's Elizabeth's father. I can be furious with him—especially after what he did to Spider—but I can't hate him."

Mick glanced across at her. "How do you feel about meeting his fiancée?"

"I don't know." Silent for a moment, Maggie tried to decide what her emotions were. "I don't know a thing about her," she said finally, "but I'm worried for her."

"Are you going to warn her about Bratton?"

"I might," she said, making up her mind to do exactly that.

"Now look," Mick began sternly, "you're welcome to feel as protective of the rest of the world as you like, but not until we've taken care of our own business tonight. Do you understand? Don't scare her off until we've got the pictures in hand. Hold off on the heart-to-heart girl talk until another day."

"What if I never get another chance to talk to her?"

"Maggie," Mick said, his patience running out, "think of yourself for once, will you? You're the one who's in trouble at the moment. Put your milk of human kindness on ice just for a couple of hours."

"I can't help the way I am."

"Tonight, you're going to have to."

Alert to the change in his tone, Maggie asked, "What do you mean?"

"I haven't told you about the most important role you have to play tonight."

She swallowed nervously. "I have a role to play?"

"I want you to cause a diversion at this party."

"A diversion?"

"Yeah, you know. When the commandos blow up a bridge, they always send a few guys to cause a diversion somewhere else to distract the enemy. Tonight, you're the diversion."

"What do you expect me to do?"

He shrugged. "That's your angle. Sing a song. Dance. Do a striptease or some—"

"I can't do that!"

Mick laughed. "I didn't mean a real striptease. I just—"

"Mick, I'm not the kind of person who can—can cause any kind of distraction at a party! I'm naturally shy! I—I blush if I accidentally raise my voice in a crowded room! Please, I can't—"

"Yes, you can. I've seen a different side of you than the rest of the world, Miss Margaret. Let down your inhibitions a little, that's all I'm suggesting. Just cause a small riot.''

"I can't!"

"Yes, you can," Mick soothed. Chuckling, he added, "In fact, I bet you're going to like it."

The party was well underway when Mick and Maggie arrived. Maggie clutched Mick's arm and knocked on the door.

Ben opened it, and his welcoming smile froze the instant he recognized Mick looming in his doorway. "My God—"

"Hello, Ben," Maggie said smoothly. "I know it's terribly gauche of us, but we simply couldn't resist coming. Do you mind?"

Ben didn't have time to answer. Mick had only to touch his chest for Ben to take four giant steps backward. "See here," he began. "You can't burst in here like this—"

"Who's bursting?" Mick asked. "We're doing this nice and politely, right, Maggie? You wouldn't want to call the cops and ruin your little bash, would you?" The threat didn't have to be spoken. One look at Mick's face could convince anyone that he'd make a hell of a fuss if anyone tried to stop him.

Ben coughed. "Uh—"

"We'll behave," Maggie promised.

She entered the apartment and thrust her wrap into Ben's arms. Mick was half a step behind her, and he closed the door once they were inside.

Ben didn't have much choice. He fumbled the wrap, but he recovered his charm. He even managed to kiss Maggie on both cheeks, continental style. "Well," he began, "I guess I'm glad you came. Does this mean there's no hard feelings?"

Mick intervened, disengaging Maggie's hand from Ben's. "Don't press your luck, partner."

"Ben, this is Mick Spiderelli," Maggie said hastily, holding her position between the two men just in case fisticuffs broke out. "I don't believe you two were properly introduced when we last met."

"Uh, no," said Ben, and he didn't offer the customary handshake. Mick didn't extend his hand either. "Glad to meet you, Mike," Ben said stiffly. "Now that you're here, how about a drink? Champagne? A cocktail?"

"Got any beer?" Mick tugged at the collar of his starched shirt. "I could use a brew right now."

"Uh, I'm not sure." The doorbell saved Ben from personally seeing that they were taken care of. With relief, he gestured them into the apartment. "Why don't you check at the bar? It's set up in the dining room. Maggie can show you the way, I'm sure."

Maggie steered Mick out of the foyer. "Be careful," she warned. "Your homicidal side is showing."

"I couldn't help it," Mick replied out of the side of his mouth. "*You* didn't have to be so damned friendly."

"This is a party, for crying out loud. Was I supposed to bite him?"

"Save that thought," Mick muttered in a husky undertone. "You can try it out on me later."

Maggie laughed.

Ben's glass and chrome dining room had been converted into a makeshift bar by the catering company. Two waiters in short black jackets floated among the guests, carrying sparkling silver trays. A group of elegantly dressed couples milled around the room, chatting pleasantly. But what stunned Maggie most of all was the obvious cost of everything in sight. Fresh flowers abounded. The sparkle of fine crystal, immaculate white linens and discreet service all combined to provide a gracious atmosphere that had clearly cost a small fortune. Music wafted in from the next room, a live string quartet playing something soft and classical.

Mick leaned close and said, "Bratton didn't waste any time spending your money, did he?"

"Be quiet," Maggie replied under her breath. "If I paid for this party, I'm going to enjoy it."

"Okay. Shall I get you a glass of champagne?"

"Please."

"French, of course. And some caviar to go with it?"

"Caviar!" Maggie squeaked.

Mick nodded in the direction of the buffet table. "Only the best. Do I detect a few other expensive delicacies, too?"

Maggie clenched her fists. "Okay, you've convinced me. When do I start my diversion?"

"Soon," said Mick. "First let's mingle. I want to see how you highbrows have a good time."

Maggie tried her best, but she didn't have the courage to enjoy herself. After Mick brought the champagne, they joined a group of guests and introduced themselves. One gentleman identified himself as the administrative assistant to a high-powered senator. One of the women appraised jewelry for a New York auction house. Another, whose face was familiar, admitted modestly that she was an actress and had been playing a small part in one of the nighttime soaps for three years. Another somber fellow was identified as the lead guitarist of a popular rock and roll band, though he could have been an English lord judging by his sartorial splendor.

"Interesting guest list," Mick murmured when they had five seconds alone. "All friends of the fiancée, too. I wonder where she is?"

The words were just out of his mouth when the woman in question made her entrance. Ben entered the room with a dazzling blonde on his arm. She was nearly six feet tall, wore her short hair in modified spikes and carried herself like an Amazon priestess. The heels on her shoes were five inches high at the very least, and her hot pink dress was formfit-

ting and nearly transparent. She was not wearing under-
clothes.

Mick let out a low whistle of astonishment.

"My heavens," said Maggie, suddenly light-headed.

"I'll bet that babe doesn't need to be warned about anything," Mick said. "Whew!"

She had a big, friendly smile, though, and the other guests
seemed truly delighted to have her in their midst. Ben strut-
ted proudly at her sight, clearly dazzled by the air of glam-
our and confidence she exuded. Her name was Seraphina
Vanderkine.

"Hi," she said to Maggie, when Ben introduced them.
Her handshake was athletic, her eye contact direct. "Glad
to meet you. Benny's mentioned you from time to time.
Who's this?"

Maggie turned to Mick. "May I introduce Mick Spiderelli? Seraphina Vanderkine."

"Hel-lo," said Seraphina, sliding her hand around Mick's
arm and squeezing. "My, my, you're a strong boy, aren't
you?"

"Uh," Ben said, "Mike's a friend of Maggie's, you see,
Sera. He's—"

"He's taken, you mean," Seraphina finished. "Too
bad." She puckered her luscious lips into a pouting kind of
kiss and shot it at Mick. "We could have gotten to know
each other better."

"No reason why we can't do that," Mick responded,
smiling indulgently down at the formidable woman. He was
her equal, and they both knew it.

"Uh," Ben said uncomfortably, "how about a drink,
Seraphina?"

"Sure," she said, not taking her glittering eyes off Mick
for an instant. "Get me a beer, Benny. I want to talk to these
two."

Ben scuttled away, and Maggie suddenly felt the need for small talk. Striving to be polite, she said, "You and Ben make such a—an interesting couple, Seraphina. You're not at all what I expected."

Seraphina tore her gaze from Mick and smiled at Maggie. "You mean I'm not a sap?"

Maggie choked on champagne, but Mick came to the rescue. "I think that's exactly what Maggie was thinking," he said lightly. "But she tries to use euphemisms whenever possible. You know what you're getting into?"

"With Benny?" Seraphina grinned. "Sure, I do. Let's take a walk on the balcony, okay? I want to make sure of a couple of things with you, Maggie."

"If you don't mind," Mick said, "I'll sit this one out. You two run along."

Seraphina wound her arm through Maggie's and winked at Mick. "Don't run away," she warned.

Startled, but game, Maggie strolled out onto the balcony with Seraphina. The night was cool, but she was too curious to refuse a moment alone. Seraphina sauntered to the railing, then turned and leaned against it, eyeing Maggie consideringly, but with a smile.

"Well?" she asked. "You have anything I ought to hear?"

"I'm not sure," Maggie said. "I have a feeling you already know everything."

Seraphina had a big laugh. She threw her head back and showed her teeth. "Yeah," she said. "My grandmother used to warn me about guys like him." She shrugged. "But I think I'm safe."

"Safe?"

"Sure," said the Amazon. "My family's fortune started with tobacco. We've got money to burn—it's our family motto. Get it?"

Maggie laughed weakly.

Seraphina shrugged. "I've dated all kinds of men. I like men a lot. And most of them want a chunk of my dough. So what?"

"I—I beg your pardon?"

"I mean, I've got enough to spread around and still have sufficient funds left to buy tickets to see a Grateful Dead concert once in a while, you know? It took a while, but I finally figured it out. Why worry about losing money to a jerk? Money's not important. What's important is having fun. And I have fun with Benny."

"Really?"

Seraphina laughed at Maggie's incredulous tone. "Yeah," she said confidently. "I do. He can be a nerd sometimes, and he's unbelievably greedy in nine situations out of ten, but he's basically an okay guy. You know?"

Maggie nodded. "Yes. I do know."

"He's not going to set the world on fire with his brains, but he's nice to look at, and he doesn't want to get ahead in some crummy nine to five job that'll keep him away from home half the time. I want him around to have a good time with. We'll go to polo matches, take my daddy's boat around the world, enjoy life! What the heck."

Maggie smiled. "It sounds like you've got your life very well in hand."

"I think so. But," she added, "maybe you can tell me something different. How come you and he broke up? Did the hunk show up in your life?"

Maggie shook her head. "No, Mick came along much later. Ben and I—well, it's a long story." Maggie realized she had nothing to lose. And she didn't imagine that anything she had to tell Seraphina about her fiancé was going to change her mind about marrying Ben. So Maggie told her.

When she was finished, Seraphina was more amused than outraged. She even chuckled. "That sneaky little fink! So you're supposed to stage a diversion while Mick steals the photos out of Benny's bedroom?''

"If they're *in* Ben's bedroom."

"There's only one way to find out," Seraphina shot back, her eyes alight with mischief. "Let me help."

"You!"

"Sure. Listen, diversions are one of my best things. How about it?"

"Well," Maggie began uncertainly.

Seraphina snapped her fingers. "I've got it! A cat fight!"

"I beg your pardon?"

"You know, plenty of hair pulling and eye scratching and—"

"Wait a minute," Maggie backed up several paces. "Your offer is very generous, but—"

"You bitch!" Seraphina suddenly screamed, loud enough to be heard in the next county. With a voice that could shatter glass, she shrieked, "I'll teach you to keep your hands off my man!"

And with that, she flung herself at Maggie with claws bared.

Eleven

Mick took a quick inventory of the guests, made special note that Bratton was occupied in arguing with a waiter in the dining room, and decided that the coast was clear. He slipped into his cat burglar stance and made straight for the bedrooms.

Ransacking was one of the more fun parts of his old job. Mick supposed it stemmed from every little boy's fantasy of wrecking the house while Mom was away. But ransacking without drawing attention to himself was going to be tricky. He started in the room he guessed was Ben's—the red satin coverlet over the king-sized waterbed was a dead give away—and went through all the drawers and closets with care.

He hit paydirt in the nightstand. An oversized manila envelope was filled with glossy photographs. Mick thumbed through them just to make certain he'd found the right ones. Sure enough, each picture depicted Maggie looking frightned and uncomfortable. One glance was enough to send a clenching kind of anger straight into Mick's belly. Suddenly he wanted to strangle Ben Bratton.

He shoved the photos back in the envelope and stowed the whole package in the breast pocket of his jacket.

He turned to go, but a loud noise from the living room stopped him. Listening tensely, Mick next heard a female shriek, more crashes and the shouts of startled guests. Mick grinned to himself. Whatever diversion Maggie had hit upon, it was clearly working.

With a few more minutes at his disposal, Mick returned to his search. He flipped back the mattress, tore through the shoe boxes lined up in Ben's closet, rifled the wardrobe. In the cabinet under the bathroom sink, Mick hit the jackpot.

"I'll be damned," he muttered.

Nearly a hundred thousand dollars in cash still wrapped in parcels had been stashed between the toilet brush and a stack of deodorant soap cakes.

"What's the matter, Ben?" Mick muttered to himself. "Don't you trust banks? Afraid the IRS will get wind of your undeclared income?"

Chuckling, Mick emptied the wastebasket onto the floor and began to fill it with packets of money.

Maggie screamed. Seraphina, definitely a method actress, had a death grip on her hair and was hauling her body across the living room rug towards the fireplace, clearly intent on sending her up in smoke. Horrified party guests scattered. A jostled waiter dropped a full bottle of champagne, sending slippery foam all over the floor. Seraphina lost her footing and crashed down. Maggie wrestled to get free.

"Come on!" Seraphina hissed in her ear. "Put up a fight for god's sake! We've got to make this believable!"

"I'm *trying*!" Maggie wailed.

Seraphina staggered to her feet. For the benefit of their audience, she bellowed, "I'll kill you if you so much as touch him!"

Humiliation was Maggie's reaction. She prayed for an earthquake. A fire. A UFO landing—anything that might divert attention! Desperately, she tried to tear free, but managed only to rip the sleeve of Seraphina's dress completely off. She stared at the material left dangling in her hand, appalled by her own actions and the awful melodrama unfolding without a single bit of help from her. She dropped the sleeve hastily to the floor.

"I'll get you for that!" roared her adversary. And Seraphina wound up for a roundhouse punch.

At that instant, Ben Bratton flung himself into the fray. Red-faced and sweating, he seized Seraphina in a headlock and dragged her back.

"Stop it, you two!" he cried. "Please, please, don't spoil my rug!"

"Your rug?" Maggie shouted in disbelief. "Your *rug*? Why, you—"

She couldn't stop herself. One minute she was a frightened young woman who'd been attacked by a she-devil, and the next moment she could not control her rage. She nearly flew at Ben then and there, but she remembered in the nick of time that she was, above all things, a lady. Ladies did not strike *anyone* in anger.

So Maggie did the next best thing. She picked up a bowl of caviar and hurled it straight at Ben Bratton's head. Unfortunately, she missed and hit the mirror hanging just behind him. The bowl shattered and caviar rained down upon everyone within range.

Seraphina, madness in her eye, screamed, "Food fight!"

The whole party went berserk.

Maggie was about to arm herself with a dish of vegetable dip when someone grabbed her from behind, pinning her arms and hauling her backward and out of the battlefront. She struggled and fought, kicking as hard as she could.

"Ow!" Mick cried. "For crying out loud, I said a *diversion* not a world war!"

"Mick!"

He was laughing and trying to duck whatever projectiles zoomed past his head at the same time. "By God, you're the woman for me, Miss Margaret! You've been watching those old commando movies after all, haven't you?"

"I've done my part," Maggie shouted above the bedlam. "What about you?"

In triumph, Mick held up a trash basket which made no sense at all. He was smiling, though, so Maggie figured she could trust him.

"Let's get out of here!" he said.

"Do you think Ben will notice we're gone?" Maggie asked.

"I don't think so. He looks indisposed at the moment," Mick shouted above the din. "Someone just dunked his head in the punch bowl!"

Heads down, they skidded for the door and managed to get themselves out into the hall and down the steps. Laughing giddily, they ran across the parking lot. In the car, Mick upended the trash basket and filled Maggie's lap with money.

Overjoyed, she threw her arms around his neck. "Kiss me!"

He obliged, but asked, with his most wicked of grins, "If a hundred grand will buy me a kiss, what will I get for these?"

Maggie froze for a second, and then with shaking hands she accepted the large envelope he extended to her. She didn't bother to look inside. The light in Mick's eyes told the story.

"Oh, Mick," she said. "You've saved my life."

"No," he said. "We did it together. You're one tough partner, Miss Margaret. I think we're unbeatable. Do you want to go home to celebrate?"

She nodded, tears of joy and relief filling her eyes. "Yes," she said. "And then I want to spend a very long time thanking you."

"My boat's tied up not far from here," he said, leaning close to kiss her mouth. "We could be back at the villa in a matter of days."

"Now that," said Maggie, weak with happiness, "would be a celebration indeed."

Epilogue

The Caribbean was no less beautiful by night than by day. Moonlight danced on the silvery crests of the incoming surf. The wet rocks gleamed, and beyond them stretched the huge curving ribbon of beach. The Kincaid villa was above, nestled in the trees and as Mick sat on the rocks in the darkness, he watched the glow of flickering hurricane lamps on the balustrade and wondered about the other men and women who had lived and loved on that very beach. Perhaps long ago a pirate captain had prowled the rocks and climbed those walls to steal the woman of his constant dreams. Or maybe the woman had been the thief—secretly courting the heart of her unwilling lover until he could resist her no longer.

Tonight the woman came to the pirate. Mick distinguished her lithe shape as she walked purposefully up the beach toward him, her white bathing suit flashing against the darkness of the night, her lustrous hair billowing in the sea breeze. The moon cast cool beams of light down her slim figure, touching her skin as lightly as Mick's own lips had done just an hour before.

The flush of ecstasy no longer colored her cheeks, though. Maggie was tense with apprehension. Barefoot, she climbed the rocks and sat beside him.

"I woke up," she said softly. "And you were gone. I was afraid."

Mick clasped her hand between his two and kissed her fingers. "Don't be afraid. I needed to be alone."

Maggie gave a soft, anxious sound. "You're getting ready to do something," she said quietly. "I've known it since we sailed down here. You're not always good at hiding what you're thinking. Have you decided?"

Mick clenched his teeth and looked out at the gentle sea. The tide had begun to wash in, lapping back up at the rocks around them, cleansing and covering their harsh and jagged shapes. As the stones disappeared into the ocean, so vanished the dull pain Mick had kept inside for so many years. He wished he could tell Maggie everything, to put her mind at ease. But the words he needed to speak were not for her, but another woman. It was Victoria to whom he had to say his farewells.

When he didn't answer, Maggie spoke first. "You have to do what you think is right, Mick. If you need to go away, then do it. Just remember that I love you."

She brushed a kiss on his lips. "Elizabeth and I can wait for you. Just don't say goodbye and mean it forever. I'd have to come after you."

Mick took her into his arms. He hugged her fiercely, pressing his cheek against her silky hair, inhaling the sweet fragrance of her subtle perfume.

"I won't say goodbye," he rasped when he could find his voice. "Not to you. I had to put Victoria to rest."

Maggie was quiet, ready to listen.

"I loved her," he said slowly, "in the beginning. But then we grew apart and I—I wish we'd had a chance to end things properly, that's all. For her to die when we hadn't resolved our differences is— It's hard for me to accept."

Maggie sat back and smiled. "You like your details nicely sewn up at the end, I know. But life doesn't always happen that way, love."

"It doesn't seem fair," he admitted at last. "For me to be this happy with you."

"You think you ought to be punished?"

He shook his head. "Maybe. For not working harder to make my marriage succeed. For not loving Victoria after I'd promised I would."

"Perhaps," said Maggie, "you're being given a second chance."

He looked into her lovely face, and she was smiling.

"With me," she added. "Victoria is gone. You can't bring her back just to settle things. But you have helped me out of my troubles. You've given me a new life, Mick. You've had your second chance, and you did the right thing."

The weight of anguish lifted at her words, and Mick let his mouth possess the sweet warmth of her lips. Desire sparked between them, for Maggie felt pliant and gentle in his arms, and Mick's own body responded to her as it always did. No sane mind could have denied the passion he felt for her, the need to protect and cherish her, the desire to be with her tender spirit always.

"Maggie," he whispered, "I do love you. You recognized it long before I could say the words. I need you. You're the half that was missing, the part that makes me whole again. I feel as though I can get my life together again with you to help me."

"Then stay," she said. "I need you, too. I'd be such a prissy stickler for convention if you weren't here to shake me off my pedestal now and then."

He grinned. "And I'd turn into an awful slob without you. Maggie, I love you now and forever."

She kissed him then, retreating only to murmur her love time after time and caressing Mick with slow, innocent touches that inflamed him with each passing moment, yet filled him with tenderness at the same time. Bathed in moonlight, warmed by the ocean breeze and their own heady passion, they found peace in each other's arms. Laughter bubbled between them, too, for in time they heard the shouts of children from the villa terrace.

"Hey!" bellowed Spider. "Are you guys being mushy again?"

Mick sighed. "Miss Margaret, we've got to teach that little monster some manners."

*   *   *   *   *

Look for Nancy Martin's
Silhouette Classic, BLACK DIAMONDS,
coming in January 1989.

CHILDREN OF DESTINY

A trilogy by Ann Major

Three power-packed tales of irresistible passion
and undeniable fate created by Ann Major to
wrap your heart in a legacy of love.

PASSION'S CHILD — September

Years ago, Nick Browning nearly destroyed
Amy's life, but now that the child of his
passion—the child of her heart—was in danger,
Nick was the only one she could trust....

DESTINY'S CHILD — October

Cattle baron Jeb Jackson thought he owned
everything and everyone on his ranch, but fiery
Megan MacKay's destiny was to prove him wrong!

NIGHT CHILD — November

When little Julia Jackson was kidnapped, young
Kirk MacKay blamed himself. Twenty years later,
he found her...and discovered that love could
shine through even the darkest of nights.

 **Silhouette Desire**

COMING NEXT MONTH

#463 LADY OF THE ISLAND—Jennifer Greene
Getting involved with Jarl Hendricks was far too dangerous for
fugitive Sara Chapman. She was trying to protect her child, and Jarl
was the one man who could uncover her secret.

#464 A TOUCH OF SPRING—Annette Broadrick
Accompanying Colonel Alexander Sloan across the country on a
promotional book tour started out as a routine assignment for
publicist Stephanie Benson. But there was nothing routine about
Alex!

#465 CABIN FEVER—Terry Lawrence
Trapped after an avalanche, her only contact the gruff voice of
"Rescue Central," Autumn Kierney couldn't help fantasizing about
the man. And reality more than met her expectations....

#466 BIG SKY COUNTRY—Jackie Merritt
When Slade Dawson decided to seduce his father's widow for
revenge, he hadn't counted on falling in love with Tracy
Moorland...or finding out who his real father was.

#467 SOUTHERN COMFORT—Sara Chance
Partners Victoria Wynne and Cord Darcourte were a professional
team and the best of friends. But lately Victoria had been having very
*un*friendly thoughts about Cord!

#468 'TIS THE SEASON—Noreen Brownlie
Volunteering to bring Christmas cheer to an elderly person hadn't
prepared Holly Peterson for fellow volunteer Nick Petrovich. Nick
wanted much more than a fleeting holiday enchantment.

AVAILABLE NOW:

FOUR UNIQUE SERIES
FOR EVERY WOMAN YOU ARE..

Silhouette Romance

Love, at its most tender, provocative,
emotional... in stories that will make you laugh and
cry while bringing you the magic of falling in love.

6 titles per month

Silhouette Special Edition

Sophisticated, substantial and packed with
emotion, these powerful novels of life and love will
capture your imagination and steal your heart.

6 titles per month

Silhouette Desire

Open the door to romance and passion. Humorous,
emotional, compelling—yet always a believable
and sensuous story—Silhouette Desire never
fails to deliver on the promise of love.

6 titles per month

Silhouette Intimate Moments

Enter a world of excitement, of romance
heightened by suspense, adventure and the
passions every woman dreams of. Let us
sweep you away.

4 titles per month

SILG-1R